Second Sun

MATTHEW R. SMITH

ISBN: 0692372482
ISBN-13: 978-0692372487

FOR LINCOLN

Always follow your dreams
and never let anyone
tell you
you can't.

Thank you to everyone involved who made this story a reality. A special thanks to my wife, Jennifer, who never let me quit and made sure I dotted every t and crossed every i.

iii

Sometimes, what's inside of you is bursting to get out. Thoughts, emotions, feelings. Like water rushing out of a faucet. The power is there. You just have to set it free.

ONE

"Wait! Stop right there!" The guard chasing me this time was a huge mass of a human. He looked more like a giant statue that you would spot swinging a baseball bat outside one of those stadiums that used to be in every major city in the United States.

The Dodgers; that was my team back then. I remember going to the games with my dad every summer. We would both get a Heart Attack Hot Dog and a large soda. I never could finish all of mine, but Dad seemed to know that because he always devoured my leftovers. "You gonna finish that?" he would say. I always eyed the cotton candy vendor walking up and down the bleachers but I was too full to even think about eating anything else. What I would give for even a morsel of the sugary substance now. Heck, I would even take some of the pink, even though the blue was always my favorite.

My leg was throbbing with pain from the hole I just crawled out of. We weren't supposed to be out at night but I had been scrounging for any metal I could find to repair the stove. I had totally forgotten about curfew and now I only had a few minutes to get across the city.

I can't believe what all I've been through since my parents were taken by the C.O.R.P.S.E. last year. I've done a lot of growing up since then; more of a necessity than anything else. My sister, who is older than me, but not by much, is always telling me to grow up. She says, "Charley! Why can't you be more like me? We would be better off if you'd just listen to me!" I'm not exactly sure what she means since we are both exactly the same age. We look just like each other and even wear some of the same clothes; well, we do now anyway...

My family lived in a large apartment building right in the middle of the city. We were so lucky back then. Our parents provided us with everything we ever wanted. I never really knew how fortunate we were. It's kind of like those times when you see a homeless guy on the street begging for money. It always made me stop and think about what that would be like. It never stayed with me very long. Just a passing thought and then on with my day. Until one day. THE day. That was the day that changed everything. Everyone's idea of normal was gone. My television, gone. My entire bedroom, gone. Man, I miss my bedroom.

My dad was a scientist and always brought me any computer parts lying around his lab.

My room was full of hardware from floor to ceiling. I think I learned more in my room than I ever did at school. Not that I didn't enjoy school. I did. I guess it was just that when I was in my room, by myself, I could really let my imagination fly. The last thing I remember programming was a small robot that would feed my goldfish for me every morning. It worked pretty well until one day when the power went out and I forgot to check the fish tank for a while.

The guard had finally given up trying to catch me and went back to doing whatever it is they do when they aren't chasing us.

Panting hard and almost crippled from falling in that hole, I finally reached my home. Our home I guess I should say. It's where my sister and I have been staying for almost a month now. It's actually one of the longest stretches we've stayed in one place since we lost everything.

Climbing down the makeshift ladder I had built from left over PVC pipes, I called to my sister. "Beka! Whatchya making for dinner?" She was back from scavenging for the day and had started cooking. She never stayed out long. She always ended up getting frustrated and came home quickly. That was fine with me because I was always starving after a long day in the city. Her cooking smelled amazing. She could turn the worst scraps I found that week into a gourmet meal. My sister was a really good cook thanks to my mom being a chef and all.

Every Friday night we would go down to my mom's restaurant, "Les Poisson." Fish wasn't my favorite food in the world, but my mom could make anything taste like the best thing you had ever eaten. "Welcome friends!" That's what my mom would say every time we entered the kitchen. It didn't matter who was coming to see her, she always said welcome friends. I never really thought anything about it until my buddy, Rider, came to eat with us one night. "Hey Charley," he asked, "why does your mom call you a friend when she's your mom?" I always meant to ask her that but just never got around to it. We always came in the back door since the main restaurant was packed most of the time with hungry families. We could eat whatever we wanted as long as we stayed in the kitchen. I don't think I ever ate at a table. In fact, I can't really remember what the restaurant looked like.

Our home, if you want to call it that, wasn't much more than a hole in the ground. My sister had dressed it up the best she could. She said that if we couldn't have nice things anymore that she would, "at least make the place livable." It never really mattered to me what the place looked like. The important thing was that we were safe. The room did give off a cozy feeling, not that I told my sister that. She could cry at the drop of a hat when anything got the least bit sentimental.

This place we decided to call home for now basically consisted of a rectangular room that used to be part of an old train station. Years ago, some developer had come through and turned the station into an apartment building of sorts. It was basically half walls that didn't reach all the way to the ceiling. We had "acquired" one of these apartments and since then have fought tooth and nail to hang on to it. I guess you could call us one of the lucky ones.

Since the walls were so short, you could hear everything that went on in all of the apartments throughout the station. And I mean everything. It didn't surprise either of us anymore to hear an ear-piercing scream coming from somewhere in the middle of the night. I don't think I slept more than an hour at a time for the first week or so. The strange thing is, whatever was going on somewhere on the other side of the station, never seemed to reach our end. I don't know if it was good fortune or just good planning, but we have never been in the middle of one of those late night horror stories. I still get chills thinking about them. Those are the times when I wished more than anything that my dad was still around. He always knew what to say when I was scared. I didn't even have to tell him I was frightened; he could just sense it.

My dad was the type of guy that would do anything and fix anything for anybody. If he didn't know how to fix it, he would learn all he could to make sure he could repair it the next time. He was one of those people that never gave up and fought to the last minute. Anyway, I don't really like talking about my parents all that much. They worked really hard to make sure me and my sister would be safe when they weren't around anymore. They knew since they only had two kids that it wouldn't be long before we would need to survive on our own. The Ones In Charge didn't look too kindly on families with only two children. Three, four, five?

Now those were the families living it up. Those were the families still together. In this place, you were better off not having any children at all. One or two would get you sent away. That was a topic that my sister and I talked about quite a bit. Especially at night when the screams started. It was something to take our minds off it.

"Where do you think they took them?" Beka asked.

"I always picture them sitting on a small island drinking sweet tea and chowing down on a hot dog," I said.

The only thing that really kept us going was to imagine our parents still alive and waiting somewhere for us. We knew there was absolutely no way for them to ever reach us. Just the thought of them planning a rescue mission was absurd. The C.O.R.P.S.E. had fortified the city where we were living with walls so high you couldn't see the top. I remember going to New York City once and seeing the Empire State Building. That was an amazing sight, but at least I could see the top. I've never seen something so massive as the walls surrounding this city. The amazing thing to me is how quickly the walls were built. It seemed like one day they were just…there. One hundred and forty-eight square blocks. We were surrounded in what seemed like a few days.

Of course that wasn't the case. We knew what was happening for a while. It was just that I was so busy trying to survive those first few weeks while not losing my sister in the process, that I lost track of time and what was really happening around me.

I remember seeing a television show once about people trying to stay alive in dangerous situations. The narrator called it a "survival instinct." I think I now know what he meant. Your body and mind sort of switch on this extra power that you never knew you had.

Don't get me wrong, I was dead tired every night after a day of looking for food and shelter while avoiding the guards and worrying about what my sister was doing or if she would even make it home. It was just that during the day, during my endless searching, my whole self went into this hyper mode that allowed me to do some amazing things.

Those first days felt like a blur. I barely remember the trucks pulling up. I can't even remember what color they were or what they sounded like. All I do remember are all the kids running after them. Screaming for their parents to come back. I remember seeing all the moms shaking the cages that covered the trucks. Shaking them so hard the bars would rattle. They were trying everything to get off the trucks and run back to their children. It was hopeless. So many young children. Four and five year olds on their own without their parents. Who was going to take care of them? Would they even survive? What was the point of all this? Those questions ran through my head for days. They would have driven me crazy if it hadn't been for my sister. She kept on saying the same thing over and over. "Charley, we will be okay. They are just taking them out of the city to get a place ready for us to live." I knew that she was lying to me but it somehow helped to think that they wanted to go, not that they were forced to. I eventually made myself turn off the images in my mind. It was like flipping a switch. One day it was all I could think about. Where had they gone? Why didn't they come back for us? And then I turned it off. Like a faucet that was gushing water and then is suddenly shut off at the main. Done. Off. I couldn't dwell on it any longer.

When the last of the adults, anyone over the age of eighteen, were finally forced out of the city, beyond the walls, we knew we were on our own. We had arrived here as a family and now all that was left were brothers…sisters…only children. Any families with less than three children were invited to live in this "New City." They said it was to keep the population down. They said it was going to be a fresh start for us "lucky few."

They lied.

They lined us up like pigs heading for slaughter. Each one of us counted, tagged, and sent away to fend for ourselves. Each one of us adding a "plus one" to the total on the wall. The number on my shoulder still burns from the hot iron. I can still feel the individual digits emblazoned on my arm. One thousand, two hundred, twenty two. My sister, of course being right in front of me, got one thousand, two hundred, twenty one.

After she stopped crying I remember her saying, "That's okay, at least mine is a palindrome." Whatever that was. My sister was always the optimist in our little twosome.

I will never forget the sound of all of those kids lining up to be numbered. Most of the older kids were trying to act tough. A few let out a whimper here and there. It was the little ones that were hard to watch.

Three thousand, five hundred, twenty nine kids. That's how many of us were left according to the wall. Trapped inside this living, breathing, nightmare. The wall. The large display screen on the south end. The size of a city billboard. Showing the number. Blasting the number in bright red lights. Bright enough to see your way at night. Bright enough to burn the image into your brain. Day after day. Three thousand, five hundred, twenty nine.

That is until this day.

This is the day the account changes. This is the day of the remaining. The day the sign changed our lives forever. Three thousand, five hundred, twenty nine. 3,529…3,529… I could read it forward, backward, and upside down. Until that day. The day my sister and I will never forget. The day the sign started to count backward.

TWO

The city was eerily silent on the morning the countdown began. Usually after the bell rings the streets are full of kids. Most of the kids I saw at sunup didn't even seem to notice the numbers changing. We had been there so long. Day after day, week after week. It felt like forever. Like this was the only thing that had ever been. A lot of them never even bothered to keep up with the date anymore. Once the last of the parents were finally forced out, days of the week became a thing of the past. Each day was focused solely on searching and surviving. I was going to wait to talk to my sister after she woke up but I couldn't hang around any longer. I had to get started for the day. Exploring the city was the only good part of my day but it took forever.

I always thought walking around an enormous city by myself would be exciting. It turned out to be a chore much worse than anything back home. A skyscraper with ninety-five floors seems like the coolest thing in the world to explore. That is until you realize the elevators are out and since there was obviously no air conditioning, anything above the fifteenth floor felt like a furnace. I always tried to go to the top of at least one of the towers every day.

I knew I couldn't see anything over the wall, but those were some of the best spots in the entire city to find survival packs.

Most of the kids didn't even know they existed and those of us that did kept it to ourselves. These packs were more like small satchels about the size of a catcher's mitt. They usually contained items that the majority of the scavengers wouldn't know what to do with.

I had only found two the entire time we'd been here. One had a small tape recorder inside. I remember my parents talking about tape players, but had never seen one myself. There was no tape in it but there were batteries. I kept it, obviously, and put it with the rest of our supplies under my bed. There was also a small, red pocket knife with a cross on it. It only had two small blades that weren't much good for anything but I always kept it in my pocket. It came in handy more times than I care to remember. The other pack I found had four boxes of breakfast cereal and a cold glass bottle of milk. I wasn't sure how the milk was still cold but I ran back home and Beka and I both enjoyed a breakfast that reminded us of those mornings we used to have before school.

When our mom wasn't working at the restaurant, or what she called her "Passion Project," she was always in a huge hurry. She worked for one of the largest banks in the country and was responsible for "Mergers and Acquisitions," whatever that meant. All I knew was that she was on her phone all the time talking about "Recovery Ratings" and "Change of Ownership." She would leave the cereal out on the counter with a note that said, "Have a good day! Milk is in the fridge!" On her way out the door, she would set the timer on the microwave to count down from twenty minutes. When the timer went off we would hurry upstairs to brush our teeth and then race to school. I usually won, but Beka was never far behind.

Counting…countdown…days count up, the board counts down. I never thought about numbers like this before.

"What's the point?" Jacob said one day on our way out to scavenge. He was a scrawny boy about my age who lived in an old run down fast food restaurant across the street from the train station. We usually walked together in the mornings for the first few blocks before splitting off to search on our own. We would chat for a little while and then tell jokes about the guards as they walked by; under our breath of course.

"What do you mean what's the point?" I asked him.

"The numbers are counting backward and no one seems to care! What I mean is it's not like we're counting down to our next birthday party or Christmas break," he said. "All of that is history! All that matters now is what we're going to have for breakfast, lunch and dinner! See you later!" And he was off.

He was just like most of the other scavengers. Always thinking about their next meal, or what they would do that evening after being out all day. The bigger picture wasn't important to most of the kids inside the wall. The numbers were counting down, which to me meant only one thing.

It did seem kind of strange to keep up with the dates but our parents had drilled it into us for so long before they left. We would get up every morning and all meet in front of the refrigerator. We had a huge piece of chalkboard that we kept tally marks on. Each month was already set up so that all we had to do was make a new mark and change yesterday's date at the top to today's date. Our parents saw this as a very important event in our daily lives. That meant we did too. That habit stuck with me and my sister. I'm not sure, but we may have been the only two kids in the entire city who actually knew today was Saturday.

Since I had woken up a little early that morning, I decided to take the long way around the city. I usually went straight to a few lesser known spots before they were all picked clean for the day. The majority of kids didn't wake up until noon, which made the morning prime time for finding items my sister and I needed.

Jacob always went to the dump first thing in the morning, so I never had to worry about him following me. Beka usually left a note by my bed with "Today's Chores" as she called them. I didn't mind what she called it. The only thing I really enjoyed doing was exploring the city and looking for food, materials, and whatever other treasures I came across. It was the only thing that kept my mind off of the situation we were in. I'd never admit it to anyone, but it was really fun being able to run through the high rises in the center of the city and explore all the floors. I was always disappointed when I reached the higher, and therefore the hottest, floors that would look out past the city and over the wall. They were boarded up from the outside; blocking any view we may have of the outside world. Was it because they didn't want us to see what was going on? Or was there nothing at all?

A lot of the kids kept hope that there was something happening just outside the wall. Kids would gather sometimes at night before curfew and tell stories about things they thought they saw through the wall. One of them said they heard a car drive by. No one ever had any proof though. I guess that was what kept them going. If they thought there was nothing at all...

That day turned out to be one of the best scavenging days I had experienced since we were left here. The weather was great, and the usual stench of the city was gone for a while due to the rain we had the night before. Sunshine after a rain usually meant steam was coming up through the sewer pipes, which I didn't mind. It kind of reminded me of the hot showers I used to take at home. The whole bathroom would fill with steam and I would write scary notes to my sister on the mirror. She used to get so mad when she saw them after getting out of the shower. I would hear her down the hallway screaming at the top of her lungs.

It took me a while those first few weeks to figure out how I always seemed to find everything we needed to survive. At first I thought it was all the video games I used to play. Looking for clues and details was my specialty. It was the big picture stuff I had a hard time with. I thought I was just getting lucky when stumbling on a box of macaroni or a bag of dried fruit. One time it was an entire crate full of oranges. What was I thinking? How could a crate of oranges be sitting around for so long without someone noticing? That was when I realized that the earlier I went out to explore, the better.

It seemed like every day there were new items hidden everywhere. You could look in a post office box that had been empty for days and find a fresh loaf of bread. Search the desks of empty office buildings and find a candy bar. It was never a lot. Just one item here or there.

I knew it had something to do with the guards and our curfew time but it wasn't until one night, when I snuck out past curfew, that I saw what was really going on.

As soon as most of the kids on our side of the city had gone to sleep, whether it was in a makeshift room for the night, or a place like my sister and I had, I traveled out to a spot inside an old deserted bank and waited. Nobody ever went into the banks anymore and I knew it would be a safe spot to sit and pass the time.

I couldn't sleep at all that night anyway. There was too much fighting and yelling going on in our side of the building. I used to always tell my sister that we should move to one of the banks. That they were the safest places to sleep. She always had the same answer.

"Charley! What if someone locked us in the vault?"

I told her that was impossible since the vaults were all connected to some sort of timer. The power was cut off to the city a long time ago. There was no way we could get locked inside. It didn't seem to matter to her. I stopped asking her to move when she started crying. That was usually the end to all of our arguments.

I was about to give up for the night and head back home when I heard the strangest sound I had ever heard in my life. Stranger than when our cat ran out and got her head stuck in the flower pot. It was kind of like the sound a car makes when it's about to run out of gas. "Clunk, clunk, ggrrhhhmpp." Over and over. Almost like a mechanical grinding. I strained to see, but it was so dark I could hardly make out my hand in front of my face.

Then I saw it.

Hundreds of ropes falling from somewhere above my position. I strained my neck to get a better view. They looked like tall vines reaching high into the sky. My heart skipped a beat. I couldn't breathe. Nothing like this ever happened in the city. At least not during the day. We were alone. No one was going to save us. Ever. Was this the rescue we had all been hoping for? I almost jumped up and ran outside I was so excited.

The ropes began falling one and a time; then a bunch of them all together. All over the street. One end of rope barely touching the ground. The ropes were hanging from the sky as if coming from nowhere. No sound. Nothing. My heart was beating so fast I thought I was going to pass out. What if this wasn't a rescue? If I was caught out here at night... I couldn't think about it.

There was a story a while ago about a kid staying out past curfew. They said he had wanted to see what it looked like from the top of a skyscraper at night. Apparently he never came back the next morning. The number on the sign didn't move, but no one ever saw him again.

I slowly crawled across the floor until I could see out one of the small windows. There were bars on the windows of the bank that made it difficult to see what was going on. The ropes were just hanging from the pitch black sky. Nothing was happening. "What in the world?" I kept asking myself. Until finally I saw them. Dark figures wearing all black started climbing down the ropes. There appeared to be small green lights next to where their eyes would be. Huge bags were strapped to their backs. The packs looked so large I thought for sure they would drop them. They were down the ropes in seconds. Still no noise. No sound at all. It was as if they had done this a hundred times and perfected it. Like an art. They had definitely done this before. The second they reached the bottom they started unzipping the enormous satchels. Even the zippers were silent.

Once when I tried to sneak out of the house to go to a concert, my mom came running down the stairs. "Where do you think you're going Mister?" I couldn't believe it. I didn't even care about getting caught at that point.

"How did you hear me?" I asked.

"The zipper on your jacket Buddy! I could hear that thing a mile away!"

After that, I always waited until I was outside to zip up my jacket.

The dark figures had the bags open now. Straining over the wall, I could just make out what was inside. Food! They were packed with all sorts of food. Boxes, cans, bags of rations. I had an uncle in the military and he would always bring me a bag of rations when he came to visit. I remember him telling me how important it was for him to carry just enough food to survive for three days. "No more, no less!" he would say.

As the figures started emptying the satchels, they immediately began sprinting into the surrounding buildings. When they came out, their bags were completely empty. All that food, being hidden throughout the city? "Why? Why were they keeping us alive like this?" I asked myself over and over. I just couldn't imagine any reason. What is the point? Why would they keep thousands of kids trapped in a city for months on end? I tried to push logic out of my head. Common sense had gone out the window a long time ago. Time to focus on what was happening and not why it was happening.

"Keep focused, Charley!" I could hear my dad's voice in my head. "Stay on your feet and keep your eye on the ball!"

We played basketball every afternoon. Rain or shine, my dad was always there. I knew he was super busy with his new business, but he never missed a game. I guess I took those times for granted. I just never really thought about it. Too little, too late now.

Before I knew what was happening, the figures were back in the middle of the street; empty satchels in one hand, rope in the other. They left just as silently as they came without a trace of ever being there.

I sat in that bank for a long time. The sun was casting faint shadows on the wall and I knew I'd better get back before Beka woke up. I was fifteen blocks away from our apartment and she would have a fit if she knew what I had done.

THREE

I was too far away. I would never make it before roll call. The sun was already up and they never waited this long to signal our tags.

Every morning the C.O.R.P.S.E. sent some sort of signal to a chip implanted in our arms. It was a quick little beep, but if you listened carefully you could hear it. We hadn't had a working clock for quite a while but I could always sense when it was time.

No sound yet, which meant I was safe for a few more minutes.

Six blocks to go. My chest felt like it was about to explode. I walked all over the city practically every day, but my body was definitely weaker compared to a year ago. I played baseball in the summer and basketball in the winter. I was never sick and always full of energy. I missed good food. I missed it every day. Not because of how it tasted, but because of how it made me feel. Anything left in the city was usually stale or rotting.

Five blocks away. I was panting harder than ever. My legs were going numb and I could feel my pulse in my fingertips. I could just make out the fast food restaurant across from the apartments. If I could hang on a little longer, I could make it back. I'd make it back and nobody would be the wiser. I would have not only stayed out way past curfew, but also avoided the guards for an entire night. I never heard of anyone doing that before. Not that I would have. They would immediately take the rule breaker to the subway station.

The C.O.R.P.S.E. had cordoned off the station for five blocks in every direction. No one was allowed anywhere close. If anyone broke a rule or didn't obey a guard's order, they were immediately taken to the station. This was one mystery that not even I wanted to solve. My imagination was enough to keep me far away from the subway.

Three blocks. My legs had given out a long time ago. I was running on pure adrenaline. I was so close. Not a single kid was on the street and there wasn't a guard in sight. I thought that was a little odd, but the only thing that mattered right now was getting back to my receiver.

Whenever anyone moved to a new location, we had to take our receiver with us. It took an entire day for it to reset to your new position, so that meant sitting around for twenty four hours before you could leave and start exploring the city. Some kids would forget to stock up on supplies before they moved. Running out of supplies right after a receiver relocate was never good. You had to rely on the mercy of someone else, which I always tried to avoid.

The C.O.R.P.S.E. also required siblings, like me and my sister, to stay connected to the same receiver. It's a good thing I didn't mind being around her because we were attached at the hip, literally.

The receiver sat right beside our beds. We had to touch our arms to it at the same time every morning. This would reset our phase and give us another day before we had to be back that night. I could see our little receiver on the table. A small black box and nothing else. No cables, wires, or screens. I always wondered how it worked but would never think of hanging around the apartment all day when I could be out exploring.

No one dared to ask what would happen if we somehow damaged our box.

There was the apartment! I could see the back entrance but it had been boarded up for quite some time. I made my way around to the front of the building.

That's when I saw them. I was completely frozen right there in the middle of the street. Three guards were standing at the entrance to the apartment building. Waiting. Just standing there waiting for me to get back. How had they known? Had I missed the beep from my arm? Had they known all night and were just waiting for me to return? Where was my sister? She should have been inside sleeping. Or did she go out looking for me? These were all the questions racing through my head when I heard it. The words I never thought I would hear again in a million years.

"Hello, Son."

FOUR

I couldn't believe it. I was speechless. My throat was so dry from running that I'm pretty sure words wouldn't have come out anyway. The mere sight of seeing my father standing there right in front of me was too much to take. Tears started flooding my face and my chest had this funny feeling, like someone was squeezing me from the inside.

Another old memory was dredging up inside me. It was like seeing a dream come alive. I was traveling to my grandparents' house one summer. We had stopped by a fast food place to get something quick to eat. My parents were in such a hurry that they drove off and left me when I ran to the bathroom. It felt so strange to know they were gone and I was helpless to do anything about it. It couldn't have been more than a few minutes before they returned, but that was all it took for the panic to creep in. I felt a sense of terror inside me that I had never felt before.

That same feeling was greater now than it ever was at that moment in the restaurant.

As I shuffled my feet closer to the steps of the entrance, I could just start to make out features on my father's face. He looked much older than he had when I last saw him. His hair was covered with a hood that was attached to his robe so I couldn't see it. I imagined it was grey since it had started to turn before we left home. His face seemed tired and worn out. Like he had been awake for days.

"Hi, Son."

My dad speaking caused me to lose my train of thought. I couldn't manage to speak. A first for me.

I don't know why, but at that moment I wasn't really interested in talking with my dad. I looked around for something to take my mind off what was right in front of me. Anything to use as a distraction, even for a few seconds. My eyes, out of pure habit, turned to the board. The numbers. They were counting down faster than I had ever seen them. Never had I seen the number drop more than a few digits each week. It was now changing by the second. This was unreal. What was happening? Somehow I knew my father had the answers.

"Where is Beka?" my father asked in his sternest voice.

The mere sound of my sister's name coming from his mouth made me furious. I don't know why but I felt like he didn't deserve to say her name much less ask where she was. I immediately bolted straight for him. Apparently the guards were shocked because not one of them was able to stop me from flying right into my father's legs and knocking him straight to the ground. I didn't mean to. It just happened. His head landed on the concrete steps with a loud thud.

The guards quickly surrounded me and pulled me off him, throwing me back onto the sidewalk. I'm pretty sure they would have shot me right then and there if it wasn't for the roar of my father's voice shouting above the commotion.

"Stop! I order you to stand down! That's my son and he is not to be harmed."

I could tell I really hurt him the way he was holding his neck, sitting on the steps, but I couldn't even think about that right now. Did he just say "order"? He ordered the guards to do something? I was speechless again. Almost thirteen months had passed. All that time thinking…knowing that the C.O.R.P.S.E. had taken our parents. Taken them knowing we would probably never see them again. What was he doing ordering anyone around here? In this place?

The guards immediately dropped their weapons and backed away from me. It was the first time I had ever been that close to so many of them. Beka wasn't going to believe this.

"Beka!" I shouted out. I don't know why but something inside me longed to know if she was safe. She must be somewhere in the city hiding out. I could only wonder.

"Yes," my father said again, "Where is your sister?" "I need to speak with her immediately. It's of utmost importance."

Did my father just say "Utmost importance"? Who talks like that?

At that moment, even with endless questions swirling through my head and all the things I wanted to ask my father, I did the only thing I knew to do. The only thing I had been doing for the past year. I ran.

FIVE

The streets were completely empty. That wasn't too strange, seeing as it was still very early in the morning. I knew that my chip was definitely sounding an alarm somewhere now. I was over an hour late checking in to my receiver. Not that it mattered. My father was obviously involved in the entire conspiracy that was keeping all of us here in the first place. He not only knew I was on my way to check in, but also where we lived.

Without thinking, I stopped in front of the old theater. An eighteen screen megaplex in the center of downtown. You could tell it used to be a nice area. Tree lined streets with those old looking lamp posts everywhere. Even the sidewalks were paved with stones. Weeds and time had taken its toll.

Beka and I used to come here all the time in the beginning. We would go into one of the larger theaters and sit. We would pretend that we were watching a scary movie and eat our pretend popcorn. The theater didn't have power so we were usually all alone. We would sit there for hours in the darkness, knowing we were both recalling the same memory.

Our parents would always take us once a month to the movies to see whatever we wanted. I would get to pick the movie one month and Beka the next. We would get a large popcorn and the biggest soda I could carry. It was always gone before the movie even started. I would run back to the concession stand for a refill just in time to make it back for the opening scene. Something else we took for granted I guess.

It was different walking into the theater today. There was a breeze in the air and a low bellowing sound coming from somewhere down one of the hallways. This was one of those countless times when I would have done anything for a flashlight. My mind was saying to turn around and just leave. I needed to keep running. Maybe I could make it to the other side of the city before dark if I left now. My feet kept moving into the theater. Very slowly but with a certainty that said, "This way...I know where to go."

The farther I walked down the hallway the darker it became. The sound was very loud now and seemed to be coming from theater number four, about twenty yards away. I passed the movie posters hanging on the walls. It was always strange seeing them since the movies were over a year old and would never still be playing in a theater. I kept moving forward. One step at a time. The sound was almost deafening now.

It sounded like…a movie playing? How could that be? There was no power anywhere in the entire city. I began running at this point. Bursting through the theater door, I ran down the long hallway until I could see the screen and I stopped. No, more like fell. I fell to my knees and collapsed right there on the floor in front of the screen. My heart sank into my chest and I began to cry. Emotions swelled up in me like never before. The screen showed a family sitting around a Christmas tree opening presents. They were laughing and throwing wrapping paper everywhere. There was a girl showing off her brand new paint set. There was a boy who couldn't wait to ride his mountain bike. The little boy turned his head toward the camera. He waved with the biggest smile on his face. That boy was me. It was me and my family. All four of us on our last Christmas together.

Before I could really take in what was happening, it was gone. A flash of light and the screen went dark. Then, all of a sudden it lit up again. It was so bright I had to shield my eyes. It took a second, but the image finally came into view. It was the countdown clock on the city wall. It was rapidly dropping. What was the number? Did it say four hundred fifty? How could that be? The past year had been so steady. Never moving much, if at all. It was hard to imagine the number dropping so fast. This brought back the ever burning question in the back of my mind. It was always there but came back with a vengeance now. What would happen when the clock finally hit zero?

SIX

I didn't have time to think about it very long. The screen went dark as soon as the clock hit three hundred. Almost simultaneously, a loud crashing noise came from the projector room. I quickly ran up to the top of the theater. I stood on the last row of seats trying to peer over the ledge into the small, dark room. I couldn't see a thing but whoever had been there left in a hurry. A canister of film had fallen off a back shelf and was slowly rolling toward me. It landed on its side after wobbling around for a bit like a spinning quarter on a table. Once it stopped, I could just read the dusty label on the face of the canister; "A Home Away from

Home." I had never heard of that one before. Sounded like something my sister would pick out.

I almost fell off the chair when I heard a noise behind me. I twisted around to the familiar sound of my sister trying to get my attention.

"PSSST! Charley!"

I couldn't believe it.

"Beka! Where have you been?"

I had so much to tell her. Where I had been, our father, the screen, all of it. After running up to me and giving me one of those awkward big sister hugs, we sat down in the front row with all of our questions ready.

"Charley, I saw Dad coming toward the apartment when I got up to check on you. Where were you?"

I responded with quick phrases so that I could get back to asking her questions.

"Out exploring. Saw these guys coming down from ropes. Got caught out too late. Dad was at our home."

Of course she made me cover it all again in detail, which was really hard for me. Then we finally got around to her side of the story. The story I wish I had never heard. The story that excited me at first and then turned me into a scared little kid again. I hated it when I wanted to be brave but couldn't.

My sister changed everything in the next ten minutes. She told me about our father. What he was doing there and what the sign really meant. Of course we all had our suspicions and theories. I for one was on the fence about whether or not the sign meant children were being killed. It just seemed like too much, even for the C.O.R.P.S.E. She explained it all to me in a rather surprisingly calm voice.

"Charley, after I realized you weren't at home, I ran to the window and saw Dad coming up the steps. My first thought was to run to him screaming, but something just didn't feel right."

"Go on," I said.

"Well," said Beka, "I decided to hide in the next apartment over and since the walls are so short, I could hear everything."

"What did he say?" I asked over and over.

"He said if he couldn't convince us, they may have to launch without us."

"Wait...launch? What are you talking about? Like a rocket?" I asked anxiously.

"I don't know Charley, all he said was launch. They left right after that and I headed straight here. I'm just glad we were thinking the same thing."

"Well," I was very frustrated at this point, "we have to go find out. We've got to make our way to the front gate and see what's going on."

"It could be a trap," Beka said. "We could be walking into an ambush set up by the C.O.R.P.S.E."

"I thought of that," I said. "I don't think we have a choice at this point. I haven't seen another person except for you all morning. Something is definitely going on and we have to find out what it is."

After scavenging a while for something to eat, I finally ran across a survival pack. It was odd to find one just sitting in the center of an empty hallway. They were usually in the high rise buildings and extremely hard to reach. I quickly released the top clasp and unzipped the pack. This one had dried prunes, two cans of soda, and something very odd. There was a small transistor radio in the outside pocket. I had seen a radio like this on my father's nightstand once.

It was early one Saturday morning before my baseball game. My father had been out late the night before and was still sleeping. Being the impatient one in the family, I ran into the room and started yelling,

"Get up! I want to get to the field early and practice before everyone gets there!"

My father was sitting on the edge of the bed in a full suit and tie with a small radio in his lap. He wasn't very happy with me barging in and sternly told me to go downstairs and wait for him. I barely remember what was coming through on the other end as I was being shuffled out of the room. He quickly turned off the radio, but not before I heard the voice. It sounded like a news report of some kind. What was it again? I did everything I could to try to remember. Then it came back. The message on the radio. I remembered like it was yesterday. Right before my father turned it off. The man on the other end said, "The ship is ready to sail."

SEVEN

I called Beka over and showed her the small radio. The light on the top was very dim. It took me a while, but I finally figured out that the stronger the radio signal, the brighter it got.

"It must be the building," I whispered. "It's blocking the transmission. Let's take it outside and see if we can get better reception."

We ran outside into the blinding sunlight. It took my eyes a second to adjust. After playing around with the tuner knob for a few minutes, a voice started to crackle through. It was faint at first, but then all of a sudden the light was as bright as a Christmas tree bulb. We sat there in silence for a few minutes listening to the message. It was repeating the same thing over and over again. We both looked at each other in complete silence. Not only was this the first electronic device we had used in over a year, it was the message itself that stunned us most.

"Message forty-eight out of fifty. We leave tonight. Make your way to the main gate. Punch in code five, three, eight, one, seven, six, one. They won't let you leave easily. Head north. Look for the path marked with yellow. Follow the markings and you will find us."

"What?!" I screamed. "Beka, get something to write with!"

I couldn't believe it. My father's voice was coming over the radio. He seemed so calm. He knew we would come here and I almost missed it. This radio had been sitting there all day spouting out the same message and we find it with only minutes to spare.

"Beka!" I was yelling at this point.

"I'm coming!" Beka screamed. "I found a pen in the ticket booth! What's the message?"

By that point, the message had already started over.

"...leave tonight. Make your way to the main gate. Punch in code five, three, eight, one, seven, six, one. They won't let you leave easily. Head north. Look for the path marked with yellow. Follow the markings and you will understand."

"Did you get it?" I asked impatiently.

"Yeah, yeah, I got it." Beka said. "Let's listen one more time just to make sure.

"There is only one more time!" I stammered. "We have to make sure the numbers are right or we're never getting out of here!"

Of course Beka had the numbers right. She had probably memorized them the first time we heard the message. She checked them one at a time as the digits were repeated and then the radio shut off. No hissing or static, just dead silence. The light went out soon after and I knew it wasn't coming back on. I picked the radio up off the ground and strapped it to my backpack. You never knew when an old part could come in handy. After listening to the message that final time, we went back into the theater lobby and sat down to discuss what just happened.

"What do you think, Charley?" Beka asked in a rather calm voice.

I really wasn't sure how to answer her. I wanted to jump up right then and run to the front gate. We had the code and obviously didn't have any time to waste. I knew if I was too erratic, my sister would shut down and not want to do anything. I said the only thing that I thought we could both agree on.

"I think they're tracking us."

"Of course they are," said Beka. "These things in our arms must let them know our location. How else would Dad have known to wait for you back at the apartment?"

I put my arm up to my ear and heard the faint buzzing noise of the transmitter.

"Beka…we have to get them out."

"What do you mean get them out?" she asked. "You mean take them out of our arms? Are you crazy? I'm not about to go cutting into my arm! It hurt bad enough when they put it in!"

I sat down next to her as calmly as I could. I knew it was going to be tough convincing her to take it out. All the feelings and emotions of that day came rushing back. All of the young kids screaming and crying and the feeling of helplessness.

We were at the doctor's office once when Beka had gotten a piece of glass stuck in her foot. We had spent the day at the pool and she must have stepped on a shard when we were walking back to the car. My mom always told us to put our flip flops on but we never did. The warm asphalt felt good under our cold feet. When the doctor went to pull the glass out, Beka screamed so loud he fell off his chair.

"Beka, listen. I know it will be tough and believe me, I don't want to do it either. It sounds like we don't have much time to get out of here and I don't want to miss whatever chance we do have of finding Mom and Dad. Now, let's cut these things out and go!"

I was surprised at how calm and authoritative I sounded. Usually I was the one freaking out and Beka was calming me down.

"I can't! I just can't!" Beka kept screaming. "How would we get them out anyway?"

At that moment I slowly pulled out the pocket knife I had been carrying around for months. As soon as Beka saw it she became very quiet. I knew then that this was really going to happen. I also knew then that this was really going to hurt.

I pulled out a pack of matches that I had used a few times to see my way in dark buildings. There

were several matches left so I pulled out two of
them. As Beka watched in horror, I lit a match and
began warming up the smaller of the two blades. I
knew I wouldn't be able to take the pain away, but
at least I could get the blade somewhat sterilized by
heating it up. I thought if I went first and could get
it out without showing how much pain I was in,
there was more of a chance Beka would do it too. I
rolled up my shirt and felt for the spot where the
transmitter was sitting. It felt like it was right under
the skin's surface, which meant I really wouldn't
have to dig that far. I couldn't think about it
anymore. I began to cut ever so slightly at an angle
just below the transmitter. It was easier than I
thought it would be but hurt much worse than
anything I had felt before. I knew the "glass at the
pool" memory was playing in Beka's mind right
now. As the knife touched the transmitter, a sharp
sting flew through my body. I tried to hold back
the pain as a tear rolled down my cheek. Beka, who

I thought had her eyes closed, reached over and wiped it off with her sleeve. I looked over at her as she reached out and held on to the knife in my arm.

"I've got it Charley. Let me finish before you go too deep and we have even bigger problems."

Beka, slowly turning the knife sideways, slid the transmitter to the surface. As bad as it hurt, the sense of relief I felt knowing Beka was taking charge alleviated most of the pain. Maybe there was a chance we would get out of here after all.

"There!" Beka screamed as she handed me the small silver transmitter that had been implanted in my arm since that awful day in line.

I was shocked at how quickly she had done it. I began examining the device more to get my mind off the pain than anything else. It was about half the size of a postage stamp and heavier than I would have thought. I had never seen anything like it before. I carefully touched it expecting it to be hot but to my surprise it was freezing cold. Beka already had held it for a second so she was a little ahead of me.

"Charley, this isn't a regular transmitter. Where is the battery? It should at least be warm from our body heat."

She was obviously right but we definitely didn't have the time to get into one of her long drawn out nerd talks right now. We had to get both transmitters out and head to the main gate.

"Beka, give me your arm," I demanded.

I knew I would have to be very stern with her if we were going to get this thing out anytime today. To my surprise, she laid her arm across my lap and kept babbling about nuclear power and micro engineering. It didn't matter to me what she was talking about as long as she kept still for a few minutes. I quickly used the second match to heat up the blade. I slowly placed the knife down on her arm right next to the indentation from the transmitter. She flinched ever so slightly but went on mumbling about the differences between fusion and fission. Before I knew it, the transmitter was out of her arm and in my hand.

"Beka," I said in a low voice. "It's out."

I couldn't believe it was that easy. She looked right at me and I could tell she was holding back a few tears.

"That didn't really hurt like I thought it would," she said. "Now give them both to me."

"What are you going to do with them?" I asked.

"Don't worry about it! I'll be right back!" Beka screamed as she rushed back into the theater.

EIGHT

While Beka was gone, I made the most of my time planning our next move. I wasn't sure if the guards were tracking us or just waiting for us by the main gate. I could just imagine walking around the corner into the main square and seeing our hopes of escape crash to the ground before they even had a chance to take off. We would never be able to just stroll up in broad daylight and punch in my father's code. I would have to think of some way to distract the guards long enough for us to escape.

I waited a few minutes and then headed back inside the theater to find Beka. As I got to the front door, Beka almost knocked me to the floor.

She was running as fast as she could straight toward me. She had a frightened look on her face that said, "Turn around and run!"

That's exactly what I did. As soon as I turned around, Beka was right beside me. I leaned down on the way by and swooped my backpack up with one hand while my other hand instinctively grabbed Beka's wrist as she started to fall.

"Are you okay?" I yelled.

"Yeah! Keep running!" she shouted back at me.

I could hear the fear in her voice and knew something really scared her back in the theater. I took a quick glance behind me and saw a giant swarm of guards piling out of the theater. They looked like bees flying out of a hive that had just been knocked down.

The guards were no more than half a block behind us and gaining fast. I knew we were going to have to hide. I clutched Beka's arm and made a sharp right turn down an alley. The guards may have the numbers, but no one had explored as much of this city as me. I knew exactly where to go.

I led the way as Beka followed closely behind. The surrounding buildings were only a few stories high. The guards would have those searched in a matter of minutes. I had to get us to a skyscraper. One that was at least thirty, maybe forty stories. There was the glass one about ten blocks away. That would do nicely but I knew we would never make it that far without collapsing from exhaustion. The brick one with the huge doors was only five blocks away but that would take us back past the guards.

"Charley!" My sister was shouting at me and apparently had been for quite some time. "We need to hide now!"

"I know, I know!" I shouted back. I was getting winded and knew we couldn't keep this pace up much longer. I could hear the guards and their radios blaring a block or so away.

As soon as we turned the next corner I stopped. Dead in my tracks. I just stopped running.

"Charley! What are you doing?" asked Beka, with a puzzled look on her face.

My sister was doubled over with exhaustion. I was staring at the ground right in front of my feet. I couldn't believe I had never thought of it before. The sewer. We could hide in the sewer.

I quickly bent down and tried to remove the manhole cover. I had seen workers down in them back when we would go to the city. When it was a normal place with cars and businessmen walking to work and old ladies crossing busy intersections. "This city is always a work in progress," my dad used to say. I guess the sewers were no different. I remember seeing workers constantly taking equipment in and out of the manholes. There were always three or four guys standing around watching while one guy was down in the hole.

I tried to get my fingers under the cover but it was too tight. I needed something to get under it so I could pry it up. Right at that moment I felt a tap on my shoulder. I looked up to see my sister holding a metal bar in her hand about three feet long. How was she always a few steps ahead of me? Normally I would have voiced my frustration, but I didn't say anything this time. I just took the bar and quickly stuck it under the edge of the cover. It barely fit, but I managed to jam it into the groove. I kneeled down and began to pry the cover up with everything I had in me. The metal cut into my hands and they quickly started to bleed. I fought through the pain and pushed down hard. It didn't move. It wouldn't even budge.

"Beka! Get over here and help me!" I strained.

Beka ran over from the corner of the alley where she was watching out for the guards and grabbed on to the metal bar. Almost as soon as she started to help, the cover moved. Ever so slightly it shifted to one side and started to grind across the asphalt. The noise was loud and I knew we had to hurry.

"Keep...pushing!" I grunted.

It seemed like forever, but we were finally able to move the cover half way off the manhole. We stopped as soon as I thought one of us could fit through. As I looked down the hole, all I could see was a small ladder fading into blackness. There was an awful smell. It reminded me of a trashcan sitting out in the hot sun for days.

My job back at home had always been to take out the trash. Now, whether I did or not was another matter. I remember once, when I was totally focused on my indoor, self-sustaining garden project, I forgot to take the trash out for two weeks. I thought that had to be one of the worst smells known to man. This was worse.

I signaled over to Beka to go down the ladder. The smell wafted up around us. It was so strong you could almost see it. I noticed Beka's disgusted face and I knew she wanted to go off into one of her rants about how there was no way she was going to participate in this crazy idea. She had probably seen some special on television about the dangers of sewers or what kind of diseases rats carry. Instead, she took a deep breath, stuck her leg into the hole and started climbing down the ladder.

Half of her body was under ground before I knew it. I could hear the guards shouting behind me. If they came around the corner before we could get the cover back on, we were done. Beka was still climbing down the ladder and I knew I didn't have a choice. I started shoving the cover back on.

"Charley! What are you doing?"

She was going to hate me for this but it was the only way.

"Beka, listen! I'll meet you at the sewer cover next to our first apartment. The one where we had pizza!"

She was screaming at me now. I quickly opened my pack and took out the box of matches. I tossed it down to her and kept closing the lid.

"Use them carefully and you'll make it all the way!" I yelled as the lid slammed closed.

I knew she was still down there screaming at me. To be honest, I felt really bad about this one. I'm not sure what it was but a wave of sadness came over me and I started to cry. I was really glad the lid was closed so Beka couldn't see me. Once I met up with her on the other side of the city, I would never live it down.

As soon as the lid slammed shut I jumped sideways into an abandoned store front. It was recessed slightly into the wall which kept the guards from spotting me. I carefully peeked around the edge of the building and saw more guards than I had ever seen in one place. It was a quick glance, but there must have been at least twenty of them. I crouched in the shadow of the doorway with nowhere else to go. The door was locked behind me and if I went back into the alley they would see me for sure. As I huddled there, I thought about Beka being right below my feet. I just hoped she would start heading for the apartments before burning through too many of those matches.

The guards were getting closer now. They couldn't be more than ten or fifteen feet away. All they had to do was turn their head slightly to the right and I would be done. I held my breath as my heart started to beat out of my chest. They were all marching by in four, single file lines.

NINE

The tunnel was so dark it was hard to see your hand in front of your face. It was kind of like waking up in a dim room and forgetting where you were. No matter how wide you open your eyes, there just isn't enough light to see anything.

I knew the most important thing to do was stay calm. That's what Charley would have said if he is was here. Charley…I couldn't believe he closed the sewer cap and left me down here. If I could just stay calm, the rest would work itself out. It took a few minutes to get over the fact that I had just been abandoned down here in this blindingly dark stink hole. Just the thought of what might be lurking down here was enough for me to climb right back up the ladder and start screaming until he came back and let me out. How was I supposed to...

"The matches!" I screamed out loud.

The sound echoed through the tunnels and confirmed just how massive the city sewer system really was.

As the reverberating sound of my voice finally stopped, I fumbled around in my pocket where I stuffed the matches. The box seemed really light. It was hard to imagine more than a few matches left as I shook it next to my ear. After carefully pulling one out, I felt around the sides of the box until I found the rough side. I slid the match very gently on the box. Nothing happened. The next strike was a little more forceful. A spark flew off the match and landed in a pool of water below my feet. The third strike did the trick. The match burst into flames and seemed to grow very strong, very quickly. So quickly in fact that it was burning my finger before I knew it. I dropped the match in frustration and quickly grabbed the box again. Three matches left. I pulled another match, even more carefully this time, out of the box and struck it swiftly. This time I had a plan. I scanned the tunnel to see what was on either side of me. The sewer seemed to stretch out in both directions for as far as the faint light creeping from the sewer cap could travel. To the right would take me back toward the main street where we ran into the guards. That would be pointless. I had to go left and just hope I could figure out the labyrinth of sewer tunnels before I ran out of matches. I took maybe five steps before my next match was needed. I pulled them out one at a time and walked as quickly as I could, trying to keep the match burning as long as possible. Reaching into the box again, fear immediately met me. The last one. The box was empty now. The only thing I could think to do was light the box itself on fire with the last match. As the box began to burn, I started calculating distance in my head. The three matches…or was it four? I couldn't remember. Those matches had allowed me to travel maybe a hundred yards. I was pretty much right where I started. I could still see the faint light shining through the edges of the sewer cap like a solar eclipse.

As my eyes continued to adjust to the darkness and my mind started coping with the fear, I thought I could see something a little ways down the tunnel. It sort of looked like a metal plate leaned against the wall. The more I strained to see what it was, the more it came into focus.

I remember one time sitting on our balcony after dinner with my dad. We were staring up at the stars as he called out all the names of the constellations. It was always amazing to hear him rattle off the history behind the stars and the importance to ancient cultures. As I strained to see Merak, one of the Big Dipper stars, my dad told me to look slightly to the left of the star I wanted to see and it would be brighter than staring straight ahead. Something about how your eye draws in light. I never looked at the stars the same way again.

The metal panel, or whatever it was, started to look more like a door than just some piece of junk leaned up against the wall. It could have just been my imagination, but it even seemed to have a faint glow seeping around the sides. It was pulsing very rapidly on and off but never fully disappearing. My mind was racing. I was no more than fifty yards away. I wasn't sure I could even make it that far in this blackness. I shuffled my feet carefully across the wet floor inch by inch until I was close enough to make out all the details of what was surely a door. I couldn't believe it. The only lights we had seen for years came from whatever candles or flashlights we could scrounge up. I stood very still right outside the door. Sweat was pouring down my face and my t-shirt was drenched from the humidity in the tunnels. I could hear mumbling of some kind coming from somewhere close by.

Slowly, I crept up right beside the door knob and tried to peek through the crack. I couldn't imagine what could be down here or how the power was even on.

Just as I leaned next to the door, something grabbed me and shoved me down to the ground. I covered my face with my arms and waited for the worst. I couldn't see anything and had no idea what it was. Then I heard the strangest sound yet down here in the sewer. A girl's voice.

"What are you doing down here? How did you find us?"

I was stunned. My voice wouldn't work. I couldn't make a sound. I just laid there while she kept repeating the same thing over and over. After a while, realizing I wasn't going to say anything, she grabbed me by my neck and dragged me through the door. My eyes were still shut tight but I could hear a group of people chatting and feet shuffling around the room.

"Look what I found snooping around the tunnels!"

She shoved me to the floor and I quickly opened my eyes. The room was fairly bright with lamps scattered around and glowing television sets being monitored by groups of kids. They were watching something intently, but I couldn't quite make it out. My head was killing me from the encounter in the sewer. The announcement from the girl made everyone stop what they were doing and look over at me.

"I asked her what she was doing down here," the girl shouted, "but of course she didn't answer!"

I started to say something but was cut off by one of the boys watching a monitor. He jumped out of the chair he had been sitting in and ran over to where I was lying on the floor.

"What are you doing down here?" he shouted at me while everyone else watched.

I took that as a sign that he was the leader of this bunch.

"Are you spying for them again? They know what we did to the other ones they sent down here!"

I wasn't sure what he was talking about but I could tell from his voice that they were definitely scared of something. I slowly stood up and brushed myself off. I scanned the room quickly trying to get a head count. It looked like there were maybe twenty or thirty of them. Most were a little older than average and I didn't see any young kids.

I figured if I didn't say something now, things might get ugly fast.

"Hey, my name is Beka and I'm from the city."

My big announcement came off like a scared little girl. Which I wasn't. I wished for a redo on that one.

"We know who you are," came a voice from the other side of the room.

A dark haired boy, about the same age as Charley, stepped toward me. He had been watching one of the screens intently but now seemed very upset I was down here.

"You and that kid have been running all over the city causing us a lot of trouble. You shouldn't be down here."

I took a step back as he approached me. Obviously that was the wrong thing to do. The rest of the group rose up and started walking over. It was like a flock of buzzards swarming for their next meal. After a quick emotional regroup, I stood up straight and tried to look a little less frightened.

"That kid happens to be my brother, and the only reason many of us are still alive up top!" I yelled with more emotion in my voice than I really intended.

This seemed to shock the group a bit and they started creeping back to their original activities. All but the leader, or whoever he was.

"What's your name?" I asked, trying to be a bit more pleasant.

"I'm Hafter, not that you really need to know," he said abruptly.

"Hafter, like the street? The one by the old subway station?" I asked, still trying to be friendly.

"Yeah, like the street."

He seemed to be really distracted, looking over his shoulder every once in a while to keep an eye on whatever they were watching on the screens.

"Hey, Bella, or whatever your name is. I don't have time for this. You need to go now. We're too busy to babysit you, much less explain what's really happening."

"What do you mean what's really…"

I didn't get a chance to ask another question before the room went completely dark. An alarm started blaring in my ear and a red light over the door cast a dim glow across the room. Everyone in the room stopped what they were doing and ran to one of the screens. They pushed and shoved each other to get a spot where they could see.

Hafter, after watching all of the others cram around the screen, slowly walked over to the side of the room and squeezed behind a couch against the wall. I followed him over and he seemed to be okay with that. It was still really hard to get a good view of the screen, but when some of the group realized Hafter was trying to see, they moved out of the way a bit.

As the image finally came in to view, I realized what all of the fuss was about. I didn't fully understand what I was seeing, but I definitely understood. It was exciting and terrifying all at once. It was like watching a scary movie for the second time. You knew what was going to happen but it still shocked you to see it.

I tried to take it all in but my mind was pushing back. It was telling me "No, Beka. This can't be real. There is a logical explanation for everything and what you are watching on that screen is far from logical."

Whether it was logical or not, I was seeing it with my own eyes. The screen was slowly cutting from one point of view to the next. There seemed to be five cameras in all. Each one looked like it was attached to some sort of beam. Directly in the middle of each shot was a structure. Not just any structure, but a large, steel frame that looked like a crane. But it wasn't a crane. It was a tower. A tower attached to a large concrete pad on the ground. On that pad was the most amazing thing I had ever seen in my entire life. As the screen quickly switched to the next shot, I got a perfect view. It was an enormous rocket. A rocket bigger that anything I had ever seen launched into space. I took in everything I could as the screen switched from one view to the next. Each view looked slightly different and showed every angle, though I couldn't be sure. It was at least the size of the tallest buildings in the city. It was really hard to get a good view because the cameras switched so quickly.

"Can you stay on one camera?" I shouted out loud.

I didn't mean to, but I couldn't help it. I had to get a better view.

"QUIET!" One of the boys in the front yelled back at me. "Keep your voice down or get out!"

I definitely didn't want to be thrown out so I did my best to remain calm. I really wanted to get closer to the screen, but I knew it wasn't going to happen right now. I took a step back to see what else was in the room. Hafter glanced over as I scooted around the room but he didn't seem to care. I took another quick glance around to see if anything caught my eye. It was very odd to find an entire group of people living in the city that no one knew about. News in the city traveled fast and it was hard to keep secrets. Most news revolved around food locations or where to find a comfortable place to sleep for the night. Even something that small was hard to keep from spreading like wildfire. How had this not been the talk of the town?

After walking around the room for a few minutes, something finally caught my eye and made me stop to take a closer look. There was a large bookshelf with stacks of old comic books, novels, newspapers, and magazines. Next to the bookshelf was a sort of check-out counter with one book left open. After walking a little closer, I could see it wasn't a regular book, but a journal of some sort all written in different handwriting. There were dates next to each entry with at least one entry per day. Some days had two or three entries with a few having many more.

I quickly flipped through the pages to see if anything jumped out at me and there it was. About five pages back from the most current entry. A rough sketch of the city surrounded by the wall. It looked very similar to some of the sketches Charley had drawn. The large buildings in the center with the major streets drawn in their blocky square design. That's where the similarities ended. I placed my finger on the page and traced the wall. All the way around to where the countdown was. I stopped there and then, without thinking, began to trace the lines flowing out from the wall. Outside the city, five lines, each heading in a different direction. Each one was a different color. Red, blue, green, orange, and….yellow. Yellow! The message! My mind immediately rushed back to the message from my dad. What was it? Follow the yellow path and the markings…I couldn't quite remember but it would have to wait for now.

The alarm that had been blaring incessantly finally shut off. The lights came back on and I knew I only had a few minutes left. The group that was once glued to the television screen was now starting to get up. I fixed my eyes to the page. If they were going to kick me out anyway, I might as well memorize every detail I could. The city…the wall…the colored paths…leading to where? The launch sites! Of course. I quickly memorized the order of colored paths. That part was pretty easy. The red path was near the main gate, so I made that one represent twelve o'clock. The rest were just clockwise from there with the yellow path being last, somewhere around eight o'clock.

But it was what was next to the launch sites that baffled me. Strings of numbers much too long for me to memorize in such a short amount of time. They looked so familiar though. I was almost sure I had seen them somewhere before. Where had I seen these?

"Hey!" came an extremely angry voice behind me.

It wasn't Hafter this time. It was someone I hadn't seen before. I didn't get a very good look at him, but could definitely see the wooden board being swung at my head. The next seconds were very fast and then everything went black.

TEN

"Ugh…" My head was killing me. I felt the back of my neck and it was wet with blood. At least I thought it was blood. I wasn't quite sure. My head was really throbbing and it took a minute to remember what happened. It started to slowly come back. Hazy at first and then the memory of getting whacked across the head flashed in my mind, along with the pain.

Where was I?

I felt around the tight space, which didn't take long. It also didn't take long to figure out I was inside some sort of bag. The tight space was making me nervous.

Once, when Charley and I were playing, I remember him locking me in the bathroom. I was okay for a few minutes, figuring he would come right back and let me out. After a while, I remember the panic that set in. It was horrible. I kept banging on the door until Mom finally came up and let me out. "Quit playing in the bathroom, dear," she said. I was so mad at Charley. I planned on locking him in there for good.

I felt around the sides of the bag. It could be some sort of duffle. The rough feeling of the material reminded me of my dad's old gym bag he left by the front door. The zipper was closed and there wasn't any light coming through. Listening very carefully, I tried to hear any sounds from outside. I could barely move my arms and struggled to get one hand under my head for support. The hard floor wasn't making the pain any better.

"Let's go! We don't have time for this right now!"

I could hear someone talking. They sounded really close. I laid perfectly still. Maybe they would think I was still unconscious.

"We can't take her with us! She could ruin everything. Besides, there's not enough room for her and the others would riot if they found out she took a spot."

Took a spot? What are they talking about? This was driving me crazy. Pounding headache or not, I had to know. I started to say something when all of a sudden my body was jerked up off the floor as my head smacked into the ground. I was being hurled through the air as everything went black...again.

ELEVEN

The temperature outside was definitely starting to change. The wind was picking up and cooler air started to move down to street level. The wall usually kept most of the wind out, but this seemed to change as winter approached. Since we had such a hard time keeping up with the actual date, or even the day of the week, it was always nice to feel a change in the air even if winter meant more time indoors. The seasons would come and go, friends would too, but we always kept moving forward.

Keep moving forward.

Our dad said that all the time when he was lost in the stars. Looking up on those cold winter nights, staring at the countless pinpoints of light.

"Keep moving forward you two. Keep going and never look back. You guys will do great things if you stick together."

I don't think I ever listened to what my dad was saying during those sentimental moments. I heard him talking, but I don't think I really listened. Beka, on the other hand, took everything our parents said to heart and always made sure to pay attention. I guess I never thought about a time when they wouldn't be with us. When all of those words of wisdom would actually be important.

That particular star gazing memory was rising to the surface for a good reason right now. My sister and I had separated. This was definitely the longest amount of time we had been apart in years.

I left Beka yelling at me down in that sewer more than a week ago. Since then I had been all over the city. Waiting at our meeting spot only lasted a day. I couldn't just sit there. I had a bad feeling something happened down there under the city. A place I didn't know much about. A place that I knew you could easily get lost in if you weren't careful. I was so angry with myself for leaving her down there and at Beka for not showing up. She was obviously smart enough to find her way out of the sewer. That's what worried me the most. If she was smart enough to get out, then where was she?

For the next few days, I searched frantically, going down any street that looked empty while trying to avoid contact with the guards. Everything seemed eerily quiet. Most of the normal morning traffic l was used to wasn't out today. I would normally be fighting to locate our meals for the day or making my way to the skyscrapers looking for survival packs. All that searching. I began to wonder if all of that work was for nothing. What if we hadn't gone out looking for food? What if we just sat down and waited? Would they really have let us starve? Our dad was obviously in charge. Why did he let us go through all of this only to come back now?

Once my search plan fell apart, I did what I always did when something wasn't working. I thought about Beka and what she would do in this situation. A systematic search of the entire city. I knew that was the thing to do but I dreaded it. The city itself was enormous. Soon after we arrived in the city, I had woken up early one morning to walk the perimeter of the wall. The numbers on the board were still the talk of the town back then. All the kids were spreading rumors like crazy.

"It's the number of kids in the city!" one would say. Others were sure it was some sort of lottery and you could leave if your number came up. The majority of us still felt it was a countdown to something. A countdown to what was always the question.

That early morning scouting mission around the city turned in to an all-day event. That was the first time my tracker beeped and it nearly scared me to death. I never told Beka about it and she never asked. All she wanted to know was every detail about what I saw and if there was a way out. That was a long conversation and one of the more serious ones we had in those early days.

The wall went around the entire city and enclosed almost one hundred-fifty square blocks. It was an enormous area to cover and always left burning questions in my mind. How in the world did the C.O.R.P.S.E. surround an entire city with a wall this high and no one notice? It was never on the internet, in magazines, newspapers...nothing. Impossible and I knew it. I just didn't know what to do about it.

After finishing my search at the west end of the city, I sat down at an old outdoor restaurant to mark off the crude map I made to keep track of my progress. The silence on the deserted street was suddenly broken. I looked up and to my surprise I saw a few kids inside the building across the street. It was the lobby to one of the older apartment buildings in the area. They seemed to be looking for food and didn't notice me. I finished my map and started heading out when something else caught my eye. It looked like they were struggling with some sort of large package. There were only two of them and whatever it was looked too heavy for them to carry by themselves. I started walking over to see if I could help. I could spare a few minutes but not much more. I knew I had to keep going or I wouldn't even finish a quarter of the city before dark.

As I crossed the street and stepped through the doorway I knew something wasn't right. I had never seen these two before and they didn't look very friendly. They dropped the duffel bag they had been struggling to carry and started to walk toward me. This could end up being my biggest mistake yet.

TWELVE

"Who are you and what are you doing here?" the bigger of the two boys yelled at me with an annoyed look on his face.

I kept walking toward him, through the open door and into the shop, while trying to keep a somewhat straight face and act as if I wasn't scared.

"I said, what are you doing here?" he yelled at me again and this time I unwittingly jumped and stopped in my tracks.

"Hey," I said, trying to sound as friendly as possible.

Kids were known to get beat up around this part of town for much less that spying.

"I was just across the street and came over to see if you guys needed any help. I don't get over to this side of the city much and…"

The other boy, who was kneeling next to the duffle bag, cut me off mid-sentence.

"We don't need to hear your life story kid, just get out of here. I'm sure there's a good game of hide and seek you're missing out on."

Kid? Who did he think he was? I was at least as old as him, if not older. I bit my tongue and tried to remain calm. Something my sister would have been proud of.

"Okay guys, I'll head out. Be safe out there."

I turned to go, but something was keeping me from walking away. Something in the back of my mind telling me this situation didn't seem right. I stretched my arms up over my head and took in a deep breath. My mind was running in every direction but my feet in only one. I turned back around to face both boys, who were now standing next to each other with the duffle bag between them.

"Okay you two. I'm not here to cause anyone any trouble. To tell you the truth, I've been in plenty myself in the past few days. I've been chased by guards, lost my sister, and found out that my father who abandoned us here is somehow responsible for all of this. So, I will leave and you two can…keep…keep doing whatever it is you're doing. Just tell me one thing. What's in the bag?"

The two boys looked at each other as if they had just seen a ghost. I wasn't sure what part of my statement caused this sudden change of behavior, but it made me even more curious. Finally the older, but smaller, of the two came back to life.

"Did you just say YOUR father is the leader of C.O.R.P.S.E.?"

I wasn't sure if this was going to help me or hurt me at this point, but I didn't really have a choice. My gut was telling me these two might know where Beka was, or at least had seen her. I took a deep breath, thought of all the advice my dad had ever given me about dealing with difficult people, and lied through my teeth.

"Yeah, I think I said that already. He's been in the city for weeks looking for anyone willing to go outside the wall. I'm just looking for my sister so we can get out of here. You two are welcome to go with us if you'll help me find her."

"Wait a second!" The bigger of the two boys was definitely surprised by this life changing bit of information.

"You're telling us that your dad has a way out of this city and you're just strolling down the street?"

"I told you..."

I couldn't lose my cool now. They surely wouldn't let me leave if this didn't go well. I took a deep breath and tried to remain calm.

"Once I find my sister, I'm out of here. Are you sure you haven't seen her? She's the same age as me and about the same height..."

"Okay, okay!" said the older of the two.

"My name is Blake and this is Jack. If you're telling the truth, and you better be or this isn't going to end well for you, come with us and we'll take you to your sister."

"So you do know where she is?" I asked as nonchalant as possible.

I was running out of time. The clock could already be at zero for all I knew. It had been a full day since I had seen it last. I took a quick glance outside and saw long shadows forming on the streets. It would be getting dark soon.

"Yes, I said that already." Blake stammered. "We don't have time to play games here. You either come with us now or we'll have to figure out what to do with you."

I hadn't been around him long, but Blake seemed a lot smarter than most of the kids stuck in this city. I had a pretty good sense for when someone was lying to me and I wasn't getting that feeling now. He was definitely holding something back, but he did know where Beka was.

"Okay," I said, still trying to stay calm. "You take me to her and I'll make sure the two of you get out of this city. Do we have a deal?"

"Yeah," said Blake. "We have a deal, but after we show you what we're about to show you, the only way out of here is back the way we came. You're coming with us."

I wasn't sure what that meant, but it didn't take long to find out. The other kid, Jack I think his name was, bent down and slowly started to unzip the duffle bag that had been on the floor between the two of them.

I started to walk over and Blake shot a piercing glance at me that said "stay where you are." I took a step back and waited for the bag to open. I had a feeling I already knew what was in the bag. It was the same feeling I had when I first walked into the shop.

As the bag opened, I saw the strawberry blonde color of Beka's hair. She wasn't moving and I couldn't tell if she was breathing. My heart sank to the bottom of my stomach. I almost broke down right there. My knees started to wobble and I was seconds away from falling to the floor.

"Don't worry," said Blake. "She's not dead if that's what you're thinking. We knocked her out to bring her back up to the surface. We can't have everyone in the city knowing where we are."

At this point I was furious. I didn't care what was going to happen next. Beka was in trouble and nothing was going to keep me from getting her out of that bag.

I lunged at Jack first. Flying across the floor, I knocked him off balance and sent him crashing into a row of shelving. He fell to the floor in a heap and rolled across the shop. Blake seemed surprised by this and backed away from the bag. I wasn't done with him yet but Beka was more important.

"Back off!" I yelled at Blake, making sure he was far enough away for me to safely get Beka out.

As I got closer to the bag, I heard a faint groaning sound. It was a sound I had definitely heard before.

One time back home, when we were playing outside after being cooped up all day, I ran up to Beka and jumped right in the middle of a big rain puddle. The muddy water splashed all over her pants and into her hair. She was so angry with me. All I could do was laugh and run away before she did the same to me. The sound I heard then was coming out of the duffle bag now.

"Beka!" I cried.

I needed her to get out of this duffle bag quickly. I didn't have much time before these guys realized the odds were on their side.

"Beka, I need you to wake up, like right now."

I could tell Blake was starting to rethink the situation and Jack looked like he was shaking off the surprise I had just given him.

I leaned down and started to pull her out of the bag. She wasn't fully awake yet, but I couldn't wait. I pulled her arms out first and laid her head on the floor. She was starting to grumble and it was obvious she was trying to say something.

I ran around to the other end where her feet were and started to pull the bag from around her legs.

"Charl…we…"

"Beka," I said. "Whatever you're trying to say can wait. We have to get out of here."

"No, you don't."

The voice came from directly behind me and I turned around quickly. It was not just Blake, but Jack too. They were both standing there with surprisingly calm looks on their faces. Jack was rubbing the back of his head but he didn't seem too upset with me for knocking him to the floor.

"Guys, come on" I said, trying to revert back to the calm manner I had when I came in.

"Let me get my sister out of this bag and we'll forget this ever happened."

I knew what I wanted to do to these two, but it wasn't going to happen tonight. My only goal now was to get Beka away from them and find a safe spot to sleep for the night. We could figure out our revenge tomorrow.

"We can't let you do that," snarled Blake between his teeth. "You already told us you can get us out of here and your sister has seen too much for us to let you two go."

You two? So now he thought he was going to keep me here as well?

"Listen!" I yelled, trying to add a little shock factor to my voice. "You can't keep us here! Eventually someone is going to walk by and…"

At that moment I was cut off. Not by the boys, but by a weak sounding Beka coming from the floor. She was holding her head and groaning. It sounded like she was trying to say something, but it was too faint to hear. I bent down to help her sit up and surprisingly, so did Blake and Jack.

"Grab her arms!" shouted Blake.

He seemed to be genuinely concerned for her now that she was awake and out of the bag.

I held Beka's head while Blake and Jack held her arms. After maneuvering her into a sitting position she seemed to be doing a little better. I reached behind me to move my backpack in front of me and took out my last bottle of water. I handed it to Beka and she quickly drank half the bottle before stopping.

"We…have to go with them," Beka groaned.

"We have to what?" I wasn't sure what was going on now.

"Charley, listen. We have to go back down with them. It's the only way out of here."

"Wait," Jack said in an annoyed tone. "What do you mean it's the only way out of here? Your brother just got finished telling us your father was running this place and you had a free pass out of the city!"

"You told them that?" Beka gasped.

Now she was the one who sounded annoyed.

"I had to. I had to give them something so I could see what was in that bag. Aren't you glad I did?"

For once, Beka didn't have anything to say. I knew she was glad to see me and no matter what happened, I always had her back.

I looked over at Blake and could see he was getting a little nervous about being out in the open like this. It was pitch black outside and the guards could be coming around any time now. If there were any guards left.

The silence was suddenly broken by a very feint rumbling noise. It seemed miles away at first and then began to grow increasingly louder. The ground started to move right underneath our feet.

The vibrations inside the building were unbelievable. And then the sound. It was like nothing I had ever heard before. It sounded like never-ending explosions coming from somewhere nearby. The windows started to shake violently and glass began to shatter onto the ground outside. It was falling from the buildings and exploding onto the pavement.

Beka jolted up and I could tell she knew something I didn't. Somehow she knew what was happening and I felt like an outsider again.

"Hurry! We're going to miss it!" one of the boys shouted.

It was almost impossible to hear anything. The rumbling sound seemed like a blanket covering the entire city. The next few minutes were almost instinctive. Like living to fight another day.

There was a nature show on once. The cameras were following a pack of wild hyenas who were sneaking up on a group of wildebeests. The hyenas were outnumbered at least three to one but they kept circling the wildebeests looking for a weakness in the group. It wasn't until the herd charged the hyenas that they took a step back and finally retreated. The host of the show said usually the hyenas will wait the wildebeests out until they find a sick or injured member of the group. That is unless they feel threatened. The hyenas would obviously be back one day to finish what they started.

Jack took off running, with Blake close behind him. I knew I had to grab Beka and follow them. I didn't have any other choice. There were too many questions I needed answered and the last coherent thing Beka said was that we had to go down with them. I used what little energy I had left, as I couldn't remember the last time I had slept, and pulled Beka to her feet. The two boys were already out of sight and I knew I couldn't lose them.

I could track anyone outside on the streets. The city was my home and I had made sure to explore every inch of it. But inside the buildings... that was a different story. There were way too many buildings inside the walls to explore every one of them. I was in an out of so many places looking for supplies that I didn't really pay attention.

The other place I never explored were the sewers, and I had a sinking feeling that was where we were headed now.

THIRTEEN

As stories were passed around throughout the city, it was pretty well known the one you were listening to had been twisted up more times than a pretzel. Whatever the original story, it had little resemblance to the fabricated monstrosity that was being told to you now. Many of those stories had to do with those of us who disappeared. Were they kidnapped by C.O.R.P.S.E. soldiers? Taken away to work outside the wall? Or lost in the sewers trying to escape? That was the only lie I thought might actually be true. Living here as long as we had, you were almost forced to pick a side. All of the nonsense got to everyone at some point and you just kind of fell in line with one group or another. Were we left here for a higher purpose? Did the walls keep us in or were they keeping something else out? Whatever the truth, I was definitely on the side that said to stay out of the sewers. Sure, I had used the manhole covers once or twice to gain an advantage over the guards, but I had never taken more than a few steps down the rungs of the ladder. That was one reason it was so hard for me to leave Beka down there when I did. The mere thought of trying to find my way through that maze of darkness sent shivers down my spine.

I broke for the door the two boys had just gone through with Beka's arm draped around my neck. She was heavier than I remembered...or I was getting weak from the lack of any real food the past few days. My backpack was much lighter than normal since all my energy had been focused on finding Beka and not on locating our next meal.

Pushing through the door led us into a back room behind the store. There were empty boxes lining one of the walls and wire shelving lining the other. The floor was littered with soda cans that had long been emptied.

One of the first things to go in the entire city was soda. After everyone had gotten over the shock of being abandoned in a huge metropolis with no adults for miles, kids actually started being kids again; at least for a while. The buildings were quickly emptied of anything that had the slightest bit of sugar and of course that meant every single canned drink from one end of the city to the other was devoured. Soda machines, newsstands, office refrigerators…everything. After the supply ran low, a single can of soda could get you almost anything you wanted. I heard of one boy who traded an orange soda for an entire floor of an apartment building. I'm not sure how long he was able to hang on to it, but even a few days would have been worth it. Then again, it had been a long time since I drank anything but water.

There was a grate on the floor of the back room that had been slid to one side. Cold air rushed up through the opening along with the familiar smell of rotten meat. I looked over the edge and could see a set of stairs, barely visible in the darkness, leading down into the sewer. I knew if we didn't pick up the pace we would lose them. I quickly shifted Beka's weight to my other shoulder and hurried down the stairs. This was the first time I had ever been in the sewers and knew if I thought about it too long, I might turn back. The stairs were slippery and everything around me seemed to be wet. It was a strange feeling entering a part of the city I had never seen before. I knew every inch of this place like the back of my hand but somehow it felt like I just arrived. I started to wonder how long people had been living down here. The way information traveled up top made it seem like this would have leaked out pretty quickly.

While moving down the center of the tunnel and trying to watch my every step in the darkness, I could just make out the faintest sounds coming from somewhere up ahead. I still couldn't see a thing and started to feel pretty silly chasing after two boys. I didn't even know them and they could be lying about everything they had told me up top. Beka was still a bit groggy and wasn't in any shape for questions. I didn't have time to stop and bring her back to reality.

The tunnel took a sharp turn causing me to slam right into a vertical pipe running back up to the surface. I braced myself and turned right in order to keep following the main tunnel. As soon as I made the turn, the sight in front of me almost caused me to drop Beka. I stumbled to a stop and took a minute to make sure what I was seeing was really what I was seeing. It was a room about the size of a basketball court and there were kids everywhere. They seemed to be too busy watching monitors and working at various computer terminals to even notice I was standing there. I slowly stepped forward trying to get a better view when Jack walked up.

"Go lie your sister down over there."

He was pointing to an area in the far corner of the room. It looked like a makeshift break room with a few couches. There was a television playing reruns of some show I could almost remember.

"Hurry up! We don't have long if we're going to try and make this happen, " Jack said.

"Make what happen?" I asked impatiently.

I knew what Jack was talking about, but I just needed to hear it again. I needed to know the insanity that just occurred a few minutes ago wasn't some prank just to get us down here.

"Make what happen..." Blake snickered to himself.

Blake walked up next to Jack. He seemed okay with the idea of me being down here and seeing all of this.

"You're our ticket out of here," Blake said.

I walked over to lie Beka on the couch and tried to come up with a quick strategy that would get us out of this situation. The best outcome here may actually involve working with these two. They seemed to have a pretty big operation down here that I had never heard of...ever. That was definitely saying something after all this time.

I put Beka down and made sure she was semi comfortable before walking around the room. The two boys followed me, but for some reason didn't ask me to stop.

The monitors were all showing different angles of the same thing. Something that seemed unreal. Could what I was seeing actually be happening? The screens were all focused on these gigantic rockets that looked like they were straight out of a science fiction movie. There were tubes connected to the rockets. That could mean they were being fueled right now. I didn't know as much as Beka about all this stuff but I did know they never fueled rockets they weren't intending to launch. As I kept walking around the room, I noticed one of the screens was showing the image of an empty launch pad.

"What happened to that one?" I asked.

"That was the noise we heard when we were wasting time up top," Blake groaned.

He was obviously annoyed with the time I was taking to understand things they obviously knew for a while now.

The empty pad was labeled "GREEN" on the side of the launch tower and also above the computer station in the room.

"You mean it launched?" I asked in disbelief.

Right after I said it, I knew that was a dumb question. At least it wasn't yellow, I thought to myself. If this was what my dad had been talking about in that message…

I quickly scanned around looking for the yellow launch pad. It was at the far end of the room and wasn't even being monitored. I walked over and bent down to get a better look. Everything I had learned about my father and the events leading up to this point flashed into my mind. I tried to take a moment to understand what this meant.

We had lived in the city so long now. I didn't necessarily want to be here, but I was comfortable with our situation. I knew how to find supplies and take care of both of us. I had grown up a lot in the time we were here. I wasn't just some kid going through life. I made important decisions every day. This was my home. But somehow...somehow I knew that it wasn't. I think everyone here knew this wasn't the end. It couldn't be the reason our families had abandoned us. We were here for a purpose and that purpose was starting to become clear to me now for the first time.

"We weren't abandoned here," I said aloud. "We weren't left here by our parents...this is a plan, this is THE plan!" This was all a..."

"A training exercise," Beka mumbled under her breath.

I turned around quickly.

"Who said tha...? Beka! You're up!"

"Yeah, don't worry about it," Beka muttered. "We can talk later."

She was rubbing the back of her head while giving a quick glance over at the two boys. The look on her face meant she would deal with them soon.

"What does all of this mean?" I asked, to no one in particular.

"It means we were left here to prepare." Jack said in a solemn voice.

He seemed to be sincere and after looking around I was willing to take his word for it.

"We've been here all this time so they could make sure we were ready to take the next step. To make sure we could handle any obstacle that comes up after we leave."

I was still having a hard time understanding how we got from being left here to where we were now. The words were flying around in my head. Prepare…obstacle…leave…

FOURTEEN

The last few hours had been a blur. My head was spinning and I was teetering on the verge of passing out, or throwing up. After the initial shock from seeing the underground surveillance room and learning about what was really outside the wall, I wasn't sure if I could even think straight anymore.

We were led into a small conference room off to the side of the main hallway. Over the next few hours, we debriefed basically everything anyone knew about our time here. The city, the wall, C.O.R.P.S.E., our father, and anything else throughout the past several years that could help us put together the final pieces to this puzzle. I held on to my last bargaining chip as long as possible, but even that came out in the end. I realized, along with a few glances at my sister for confirmation, this group was either going to help us find a way out of here, or we would never leave. I counted twelve individuals sitting around the table. Beka and I made fourteen. I wasn't even sure why that mattered at this point. Jake kept drilling me for more information about the rockets. He wanted to know specifics about capacity, range, fuel type, cargo holds, and every other detail I knew absolutely nothing about. This is when my precious information about the yellow path from my father's message came into play. I knew it was valuable information and also knew that once I gave it up, there would be no use for them to drag me and Beka along with them.

"Okay," Blake said in a semi calm voice. "I think we have everything we need to go."

"Go?" I shouted; not really meaning to vocalize my objections. "I mean...shouldn't we let everyone else up top know what's going on?"

"Absolutely not!" Jake slammed his fist down on the table, yelling at the top of his lungs. "Those rockets are there for one reason and one reason only. To get us off this dying planet and take us to our new home."

The room was completely silent for what seemed like an eternity. I looked around the room and tried to observe everyone's reaction. It didn't seem like anyone at the table knew what he was talking about. That piece of information had obviously been closely guarded all this time. As some of the kids around the table started to murmur and talk with whoever happened to be seated next to them, Jake slowly began to pull something out from his jacket pocket. For a few seconds, I was the only one looking at him. Even Beka found someone to talk to.

Blake walked over to Jake and held one side of what looked like a magazine while Jake slowly unfolded the other half. It was a newspaper; a very old one that had obviously been read quite a few times. The edges were yellowed and there were several tears across the front. As the two of them unfolded the paper, the room fell silent again. Everyone was now paying very close attention to what they were doing.

As the paper opened and the front page headline became visible, I knew everything they were saying was true. The past year flew through my mind like a movie being played in fast forward. Everything that I had questioned. All the mysteries and sadness. The miserable and hungry nights. It all made sense. Three bold words were written across the front page. Three words that caused our parents to leave us here and never look back. Three words that forced the world to build a training ground with no rules and just enough fear to keep us motivated. Words that somehow explained in an unimaginable way that we were actually the lucky ones. We were the chosen few fortunate enough, rich enough, powerful enough to be given a chance.

PREPARE THE CHILDREN

FIFTEEN

No one spoke for what seemed like forever. I sank down in my seat and started to replay different moments from our time here in my mind. Was it all just some sort of game? Were they conditioning us? For what? What was so terrible beyond these walls that we had to not only leave, but be chosen as the ones who were given the chance?

I looked over at Beka and could instantly tell she had already moved on from this critical piece of information and was thinking about what we were going to do next. Her eyes seemed to be fixated on the girl sitting across the table. She was staring at her clothes, her hair, and anything else she could see.

"You." Beka said in her sternest voice.

The girl looked shocked. Like she wasn't expecting to say anything during this meeting.

"Me?" she said with a sort of quiver in her voice.

"Yeah, you. Have you ever seen this newspaper headline before?"

"Oh..." she seemed a little relieved at the question. "Yes, a few times. We all were a bit shocked the first time we saw it."

"Shocked?" Beka said with more of an annoyed tone in her voice this time. "I think you would be a little more than shocked after seeing something like this."

I couldn't tell where she was going with all of this, but I just kept nodding my head in agreement. Beka then turned to look at me. Her eyes looked like they were about to blast a hole right through the back of my head. Those eyes usually meant one thing.

"Run, Charley!"

Beka jumped up and raced for the door. I was so caught off guard that I stumbled backward, falling over my chair and hitting the floor hard on my back. The pain was excruciating but I couldn't think about it right now. Whatever was going through Beka's mind couldn't be good and I had no reason to question her on this one. We knew something wasn't right all along down here. Beka just happened to figure it out first.

As I made it to the door, someone from the room started yelling. It sounded like they were talking to someone else. Someone far away. Maybe on a radio? I wasn't sure and didn't have time to turn around. As I ran through the doorway, I hesitated a little and caught myself against the wall. Beka was already out of the main room and back into the sewers. I took a quick glance around the room. The screens still looked the same. The remaining rockets were all sitting on their launch pads with steam pouring out of tubes and falling off the surface of the ships.

I kept on running; heading for the sewers. I could hear Beka yelling for me to catch up. She had gotten a pretty good lead after all my trouble getting out of the meeting room. I ran through the door and back out into the sewers. It was pitch black and a sudden sense of panic come over me. It wasn't the darkness that had me worried. It was the sound. The same sound we had heard just a few hours ago. The tunnel started to shake and dust quickly filled the sewer. I put my shirt over my nose, trying to filter the air. Another rocket was taking off. How could that be? Who was on it?

I knew now where Beka was headed so it didn't matter if she beat me there or not.

The front gates were a few blocks north of where we entered the sewer. I wasn't exactly sure how to get back to the steps in the store we had used, but I was pretty sure I could find my way toward the front gate. I reached for my pack to get out my matches. I may even still have a little juice left in my flashlight...

My pack! No! I had left it sitting on the floor by the table. How could I have done that? Just left it there? It had everything in it! I could definitely blame this one on Beka. She caught me off guard with her running and screaming.

I fumbled around in the dark for a minute, trying to find the wall of the sewer. It was cold and wet and panic again started to set in. I could hear Beka's voice in my head.

"Get a grip Charley! Use what you have and solve this problem!"

What did I have? I had nothing! Wait...I had sound! I could hear the rumble from one of the rockets off in the distance. If I was careful, I could take my time and walk toward the sound.

Keeping my hand on the sewer wall, I slowly began walking toward the front gate. Toward the sound of freedom. Toward the sound of escape.

SIXTEEN

I didn't know where Charley was. I thought for a second about doubling back to try and find him. I couldn't risk it. Not with what I knew now. Or thought I knew. If those kids down there were who I thought they were, we may never get out of this city. I had to keep going. My only hope was that Charley knew where I was headed and would meet me there.

As I climbed back up to the surface and into the back room of the store, I heard the same rumbling sound as the last time I was in this building. Except that time, I could barely stand up after being shoved in that bag. My head let out a little ache as if to remind me what happened.

The sound from the rocket was so violent, the floor was starting to crack. I knew we didn't have much time. I ran outside into the street only to be shoved up against the side of the building. The streets were jam packed with kids. I had never seen so many in one place and they were all heading in the same direction. Why were they...? No! They were all heading to the main gate! They may not know what the sound was, but they seemed drawn to it like moths to a light.

I wasn't sure what to do other than join the crowd. I knew now Charley would probably beat me there with how slowly the crowd was moving. I slipped by as many people as I could and walked quickly along the edge of the buildings. Once I saw an opening, I cut across the street and moved over a few blocks. There were still quite a few people on the street, but it was much easier to maneuver. I broke into a run and tried to make up some time.

I had a good pace going when I saw it. My heart jumped. I slowed down and just stood there, along with everyone else. I had no idea what time it was...the middle of the night sometime, but the sky lit up like it was the middle of the day. The ground began to shake even more violently than in the sewer and an intense glow of light shone brightly in front of me. Within seconds, the whole sky was filled with smoke and light. The unbelievable sound and trembling made many of the kids fall to the ground and cover their ears.

I began running. I ran faster than I ever thought possible. My legs felt like rubber bands attached to my feet. I pushed myself until I finally reached the familiar sight. It had been a while since the last time. We tried to remain in the center of the city as much as possible.

The sign. The huge sign that counted down the numbers until our ultimate doom. Or so I thought.

The sign was still on, but instead of numbers, it was flashing the strangest thing. It was showing a pattern of dots all over the screen. They looked really familiar in some sort of unexplainable way. I couldn't quite put my finger on it. I stared at the sign for quite a while even though everyone else was running around like crazy. I didn't even stop when I heard a muffled sound come up from behind me.

"Beka! Beka!"

I slowly turned around, coming out of my daze from staring at the sign to see who it was.

"Beka, where's Charley?"

It was Jake, with Blake and everyone else who had been sitting around the table in the sewer. They had obviously left in a hurry if they caught up with me that quickly.

"Listen Beka, whatever you think of us, you have to listen to me very carefully now!"

I could barely hear him over the roar of the rocket. Just at that moment, everyone froze. Directly over the top edge of the wall, it appeared. The tip of the massive rocket was towering over us like a giant wave in the ocean. It began to extend higher and higher into the sky until it was visible in its entirety. I shielded my eyes from the extreme brightness of the fire underneath the engines. It was almost too much to take as I squinted to see what was happening. The rocket continued upward, leaving an endless trail of white smoke in its path.

"Listen, Beka!" Blake started yelling at me now. "We can help you! This whole place is about to go up in flames!"

Even though I heard both of them, I wasn't really listening. The incredible sight I had just seen was holding on to me and the only thing I could think of now was finding Charley and figuring out a way to make it to the yellow path. But what if that had been our rocket? What if our ticket out of here just flew over my head? That was the strangest thing I had ever thought. Our ticket out of here? Were we destined to leave Earth? Why were we so special? Or maybe other kids here were also supposed to be on it? So many questions...

I sighed.

"Listen, I don't know where Charley is, and even if I did, look at the wall! Does the gate look open to you? Charley has the code in his backpack and only he..."

"You mean this backpack?" Jake said with a laugh.

He held up Charley's bag and started rattling it around.

"He left this back in the conference room. If you want to get out of here, you are taking us with you!"

I knew there was no way I was getting that bag from him. There were a dozen of them and only one of me.

It was either something I felt or just plain luck, but right at that moment I looked down at my feet. I was usually very confident about everything, but this situation had gotten the best of me and it paid off big time. I didn't realize it during all the commotion with the rocket, which was now hundreds of miles over our heads, but I was standing right on top of a sewer cap. Looking down through one of the holes, I could just make out a flicker of light. The flames from the rocket high above our heads were reflecting off the water in the sewer. And that flicker of light was shining right on Charley's face. He was looking up at me with an annoyed look. Like maybe he had been yelling at me for quite some time.

I moved over quickly and dropped to my knees trying to get the cover off. It was so heavy it wouldn't budge. By then, Jake had seen Charley and came over to help. Blake was right behind him and with the three of us pulling and Charley pushing, we finally got the cover to move. Stale air rushed out of the sewer as Charley poked his head to the surface.

I took a quick glance around the street to see if anyone was paying any attention, but everyone was still too busy watching the rocket fade from view. Blake grabbed Charley's arms and pulled him up in one swift motion. I was so overjoyed to see Charley safe that I forgot what I was arguing about.

"My bag!" Charley said sternly. "Give it back!"

"Whoa!" said Blake with a surprised look on his face. "I'll give it to you! No problem. All you and your sister have to do is agree to take us with you."

"With us?" asked Charley, who was yelling at this point.

Charley was getting agitated and I knew this wouldn't end well unless I intervened. My only goal was to make sure Charley and I were both safe and at least had a shot at seeing our parents again. I didn't even know if that was possible but I knew we had to try.

The bag was raised over Blake's head and with all of his people standing around him, it was too much of a risk to try and grab it.

"Listen," I said with the most even tone in my voice I could muster. "My mom always told me great leaders might not always know what to do in every situation, but they sure had to act like they did."

Charley was standing next to me and seemed to have calmed down a bit from his struggle out of the sewer. He started to speak and then paused for a second as if trying to collect his thoughts.

"Does anyone know which rocket just launched?" Charley finally asked, with a quiver in his voice that I hadn't heard before.

I could tell he was nervous about our current situation but I wasn't sure exactly what he wanted to do about it. Charley didn't wait for an answer.

He immediately started to head back down into the sewer. He had stepped down a few rungs on the ladder before I realized what he was doing.

"Charley! Get out of there! We've got to figure out what to do next and messing around in the sewers isn't it!" I was yelling at him out of pure frustration.

"Messing around?" Charley grimaced with anger in his voice.

"Messing around? This is our only chance! Do you see the gate? It's completely blocked off by screaming kids. If we take a chance and open that gate we will all die, right here, right now!"

At that moment, Charley put both feet on the top rung of the ladder and with everything in him, lunged right at Blake, knocking him over onto the ground. The bag Blake had been defiantly holding in the air went flying across the street, falling open on the pavement, sprawling the contents on the ground. By that time Charley was already on his feet standing over a stunned and disoriented Blake. He ran over to the bag, but instead of gathering everything up, he reached in the pile of items and grabbed his box of matches.

"Come on!" he yelled, grabbing my arm.

While he pushed me down into the sewer, Charley looked back at Blake, who was starting to stand up, and Jake who didn't seem to know what to do.

"Go!" he shouted with an intensity in his voice that was hard to imagine coming out of Charley. He was turning into someone I didn't recognize. Someone that I needed Charley to be right now more than ever. He was becoming a leader. I would have stopped to tell him that if I wasn't so shocked by his next command.

"We have to go now and if you're coming with us you had better keep up!"

The two boys and the rest of the group seemed stunned by Charley's demands. They all looked around for a second and then broke into a run toward the sewer.

"What are you doing Charley?" I asked impatiently. "Why would you let them come with us?"

"Because," he said with a sort of calmness in his voice. "We are going to need them to help pilot the ship."

SEVENTEEN

One by one, each member of the group
followed Charley and Beka down the ladder into
the sewer. On any other night, this would have
brought immediate attention from the guards or
anyone else walking around. Tonight was different.
It was departure night and all of the guards had
already been evacuated through the subway station.
Like many of the kids sent before them, they were
taken to another location to await possible
extraction on any remaining spots on the ships.
The guards didn't have the money or resources
needed to make the trip on their own. They had
agreed to watch over the remaining children in
exchange for a possible seat. Just the mere chance
to start a new life was enough reason to become a

guard in the C.O.R.P.S.E. or Central Operations for Research on Partial Space Extraction.

Although there was no conceivable way to take everyone off the planet's surface, it was possible, and extremely vital, that the best and brightest living among the population be able to survive. The new colony would need extremely motivated individuals to reboot the human race. These young people had been chosen for their unique abilities, some even unknown to themselves, and their willingness to adapt to whatever obstacle was thrown their way.

Like everything in life, some people never follow the rules. The rules were put in place to make sure a thriving system could be implemented on a new planet with little downtime and efficient use of resources. The rules had no regard for sympathy, or families, or feelings. The ones who chose to break those rules were the outcasts living beneath the city. They were selected to leave the city due to many different reasons but chose a different path. A path that allowed them to stay.

This group, along with Charley and Beka, were about to choose a new path. A path that would determine their fate and ultimately the fate of the human race.

That path, and the human need to stay alive, led them into the sewer down to a locked gate. A simple keypad was attached to the wall. Beka took a second to remember the numbers from their father's message and after carefully punching in five, three, eight, one, seven, six, one, the gate reluctantly clicked open.

Once through the gate, the group cautiously walked up a low narrow path. It wasn't more than a few hundred feet, but it looked like an entirely different world. The unbelievable sight before them took their breath away. Something none of the group had ever seen in their entire lives. Even the cameras in the sewer control room didn't provide enough of a view to prepare them for the sheer destruction that had taken place outside the city walls. Charred remains of cars, buildings, and roads were destroyed from fires that had long been extinguished. Street signs that once led to exciting destinations had been painted black and replaced with terrifying phrases. The one that stood out to the group more than any other read, "Take what you need. Leave what you don't. It won't matter anyway."

Shivers went up Beka's arms as she began to realize the sacrifice many had made to save the few inside the walls. Many who she felt didn't deserve to be there.

The yellow path ended up being easy to find, even in the dark. The moon was out in a cloudless sky and provided enough light to see. It ended up being a short walk around the outside of the wall. As the group walked, they saw a recurring theme all along the perimeter. Everything was burned to the ground and left to rot in various levels of decay.

Some in the group began to cry.

Others wanted to turn back.

Beka and Charley kept moving forward. They understood the importance of continuing the mission.

The path came into view and began to lead them farther and farther away from the wall.

At that moment, the ground began its now familiar shake as another rocket launched somewhere on the opposite side of the city. Everyone turned to watch it take over the sky in a brilliant array of light coming from the massive engines. The group was all wondering the same thing. Who were on these ships? The main gate was still closed and no one appeared to be leaving the city.

As Beka and Charley led the way, with the group following closely behind, a sudden sadness spread over many of the faces. As much as they were happy to finally have some answers and be free of the city, there were still so many questions.

The path seemed to go on forever. The yellow markings had stopped a while ago and exhaustion started to set in. Adrenaline had pushed them this far but with the city far behind them, it was beginning to wear off. With only the stars to guide them, the group stopped to rest along the side of the trail. As they all laid on their backs, staring up at the pitch black sky, they could only wonder what was in store for them when they reached the launch pad.

The last thing any of them heard before falling asleep was the sound of another rocket leaving the surface. As dreams usually go, the thoughts of fear, loneliness, and the blackness of space danced around in everyone's mind.

EIGHTEEN

As usual, Beka woke first. The sun had not yet peaked over the horizon, but she knew they had already slept too long. They couldn't be far from the launch pad and she was desperate to get the group up and moving.

As she shook Charley awake, the others began to stir as well. It only took a few minutes and everyone was up and ready. It was quite obvious the group had the same thoughts that were swirling around in Beka's mind. The question everyone was thinking, but no one wanted to ask. If they were able to escape the walls relatively easily, what would stop the rest of the city from following them? The rockets seemed large, but not nearly large enough to carry everyone in the city. No one could be sure how many rockets had launched...three? Maybe four? The yellow path contained one of the few, if not the last rocket left. If they didn't get there soon, they may not leave at all.

Beka was the first to start down the path, with Charley, Blake, and Jake close behind. She couldn't be sure, but it seemed like the three of them had become friends during this ordeal. If not friends, there was at least an understanding between them that they would need each other in some way once they reached the rocket.

After a few miles, the hill they had been walking up crested. What was on the other side seemed like something out of a science fiction movie. There was a path leading straight down into a deep ravine. The path seemed like it had once been well traveled, but was now grown over with grass and weeds. Looking down the path, on the far side of the ravine was a sight that made the entire group stand still in awe. About a half mile away from where they were standing was a rocket. It was the largest, most massive object any of them had ever seen. The buildings in the city were big, but this dwarfed them by comparison.

It was becoming clear now to all of them. This wasn't a rocket to just get them into space. This was a long range transportation shuttle. The kind used to travel to other planets...other galaxies.

As everyone began to head down the path, the group started to pick up speed. It wasn't long before they were sprinting as fast as they could toward the launching area. About half way down the path, Beka and Charley maneuvered to get closer together.

The path ended abruptly at the bottom of the hill. Everyone stopped and looked up at a metal sign hanging over the trail. It was a little weathered,

but the group could still make out the message
written in yellow lettering.

"Take nothing with you. Leave all belongings here and proceed
to information kiosk."

About fifty yards ahead there was a small,
round desk with a monitor sitting in the middle. It
was covered with a metal canopy and had a faded
round sign sitting next to it.

"Push yellow button for instructions."

Beka pushed the button, half expecting her
father to show up on the screen.

She was almost right.

It was her mother.

NINETEEN

She looked exactly like she did the day she left. The day Charley was screaming at the top of his lungs for their parents to please come back.

She began to speak, but instead of her usual peppy voice, she sounded stern and got right to the point.

"If you are listening to this message, then you are the select few who have made it out of the city. This doesn't mean all of you will be departing."

Everyone gasped at this but had to keep listening. There was no way to pause the video.

"Your next task will determine which of you will leave and who will need to stay. If my children are listening, I love you both and I do hope you are chosen to travel today."

Beka and Charley shot a quick glance at each other and started to tear up.

"There are twenty spots around this table marked with a number. You will find a number and then wait patiently."

Since there were more spots than there were members in the group, everyone quietly located a number and waited. Charley and Beka stood at the first two spots while everyone else filled in around the table. As they waited, a small panel opened in front of each of them and a display rose up to eye level. Everyone jumped a little when the screen popped on. The message then continued on everyone's individual screen.

"Now you will be presented with a puzzle. This puzzle will help determine if you will have a spot on the ship. If you complete the puzzle in the time given, you will see a four digit code appear on the screen. Memorize this code as it will only appear for a few seconds. You may begin. Good luck."

Sweat started to pour from Charley's forehead. This all happened so fast that he wasn't sure he could concentrate. The screen went black and text started quickly appearing. A calming voice came over a small speaker.

"Please say your full name. This will be used for verification purposes in order to access the ship."

Charley was so nervous his voice quivered as he spoke. It had been so long since he had said his last name that it sounded strange. He could hear everyone else around the table doing the same thing. They sounded so calm that it made him even more nervous.

"Voice verification complete. Please wait for your puzzle to load."

Charley gripped the table with his damp hands.

Next to his left hand, a small keyboard popped out from the edge of the table. Near his right was a joystick that looked like it was off an old arcade game.

The screen came on again.

"Your puzzle will begin momentarily. You will have two minutes to complete it. If you are not finished when time runs out, the puzzle shut down and you will be free to leave."

Charley gripped the joystick and put his fingers in typing position on the keyboard. He wanted to be ready. If the next two minutes were going to determine the rest of his life, then he was going to give it his best shot.

175

"You may now begin."

The screen went black. There was nothing on the display. Charley waited a few seconds but there was still nothing. He looked around and everyone else was typing frantically on their keyboards. They were all intently watching the screens and completing their puzzles.

Charley started to step back and then he heard it. He looked at the screen and saw his father.

"Charley, listen closely. You were always going on the ship. I made my case for you a long time ago. That's what I came to tell you on the steps that day. Only that wasn't really me. No time for that now. Anyway, I'm here to tell you that we need you with us now more than ever. Whatever happens next, you need to know that. Charley, you must get on the ship and complete your mission.

I know it sounds strange, but we are all counting on you. Whatever happens, get on the ship!"

The screen went black again. Charley had a hard time understanding what just happened. What did he mean whatever happens next?

At that moment, four digits appeared on the screen.

4 8 1 9

It took Charley a second to regain his focus. He needed to memorize the code.

The numbers were there for just a few seconds. Charley used every tool he could think of to try and remember the numbers. Then he thought of an old trick Beka had once taught him. He tried to make a math problem out of the numbers. It took a few tries but then he saw it.

Four times two is eight, plus one is nine.

The numbers disappeared and the screen went black.

The two minutes were almost up for everyone.

Charley looked around the table. Some of the kids were crying. Some were hugging each other. Charley looked over at Beka to make sure she had her number. She had a stunned look on her face. She wasn't moving. She just stared straight ahead looking at the screen in front of her. A tear started running down her cheek.

Charley leaned over and glanced at the screen in front of Beka. It was blank...except for one word in the bottom corner.

"FAIL"

The word disappeared and the screen went black.

TWENTY

"Beka!" Charley screamed at the top of his lungs. "What happened?"

"I don't know..." she said as tears started pouring down her face. "The questions were so easy. I thought I got everything right."

At that moment, the entire group fell to the ground when an air siren started blasting somewhere near the launchpad. A voice came over the intercom.

"Attention. Those who succeeded in solving your puzzle, please step toward the gate in a single file line. The outer gate will open only after your voice verification is complete."

Charley started to frantically look around for a way to get Beka inside. The only way inside was a double walled gate with a voice recognition panel on each side. Once you made it through the first gate, you had to repeat the process again to gain access to the rocket.

Charley could tell that Beka was still stunned. His dad's words were spinning through his head.

They all started heading toward the gate, with the few who didn't make it staying back. It was obvious they didn't know what to do next. They had all come so far and for some of them to leave now and not make the journey seemed impossible.

Charley grabbed Beka's hand and pulled her up to his place in line.

"Charley!"

Now it was Beka's turn to scream.

"I didn't pass the test! I can't go with you!"

Charley wasn't listening to her. His only thought was getting both of them through that gate and on to the rocket. Beka tried to pull her hand away, but Charley held on tight.

At that moment, a hand placed on Charley's shoulder made him relax a little.

Both Charley and Beka turned about to see the tear stained face of Jake. It was obvious he didn't make it either.

"Charley," Jake said in a calming voice. I know this is hard, but you have to let go. I'll protect her and we'll find another way out of here."

"You'll protect her?"

Charley grabbed Beka's arm and shoved to the front of the line. He wanted as much time as possible to figure out a way of getting them both out of here.

After stopping at the gate, Charley saw a small gray box attached to a fence post. It had a small speaker and next to that was a numerical keypad. The speaker hissed and crackled for a few seconds and then came another robotic sounding voice.

"Please enter your four digit code."

Charley quickly punched in his code and waited.

To his surprise, the gate rattled open and a light at the top of the fence turned green.

Charley and Beka both looked at each other in amazement. Maybe they could both go through.

They took a few steps forward through the entrance and the gate slowly closed behind them. There was a second, similar gate with the same gray box attached to a fence post. Charley went through the procedure again hoping for the same outcome. Unfortunately, it didn't work. The speaker buzzed after entering the code and the gate remained shut. The light on top of the fence started flashing red.

Charley, frantic now, punched in his code again. The light went off for a few seconds and then the buzzing returned along with the flashing red light.

Beka took a step back.

"Where are you going?" Charley asked.

"I can't go with you Charley." Beka said in a rather calm voice.

"I'll be okay. You need to go now."

Beka stepped outside the gate and moved over to the edge of the fence. As soon as she moved, the outside gate closed and the light went off.

Charley looked at Beka with a confused look on his face. He couldn't imagine leaving Beka behind after all they had been through. The past year flashed through their minds. The day they were left, receiving their transmitters, all the moving around, living from place to place, avoiding the guards...it was all too much to handle. Charley fell to the ground, put his hands in the dirt, and began to cry. It wasn't a frustrated cry. It was a cry full of sadness and heartache. Charley knew that he may never see his sister again.

Jake bent down on the other side of the fence. He knew nothing he said was going to make Charley feel better. He leaned down right next to Charley's ear.

"You aren't leaving because you want to. You're leaving because you have to. The rest of the group needs you. I promise you I will find a way for us to get off this planet. You will see your sister again."

Charley knew that Jake couldn't really make that promise, but there was something in Jake's voice giving him the strength he needed. He looked over at the box. Everyone was waiting to take their turn. The remaining, after seeing what happened with Beka, took a step back.

Charley slowly got to his feet and walked over to the keypad. He pushed each number in his code like it was the last thing he would ever do. As he pushed the nine, he looked over at Beka, the one person who had always been there for him, and mouthed the words.

"I'm sorry."

The light turned green and the second gate slowly rattled open.

TWENTY ONE

Altogether, nine people made it through the gates. Nine people who would have the privilege to leave planet Earth and start a new life. The ones who remained would have to find a new way to survive. A new way to live. They would have to grow even stronger than before.

Charley and eight other crew members traveled up the elevator to the top of the rocket. The trip took a few minutes, but to some it felt like seconds. Never taking his eyes off Beka, Charley reached deep within himself to remain strong. He didn't want fear to be the last thing Beka saw.

After reaching the hatch, the group carefully climbed inside. The space was quite large.

There were four crew seats in the front near the controls and a row of passenger seats near the back. Each seat had a small display near the headrest. The four digit code they had each received was flashing above one of the seats. Charley glanced around looking for his number. It wasn't anywhere on the passenger seats. He walked around to the front of the crew seats and there it was. One of the middle seats was displaying his number. There were large yellow notebooks sitting in each seat. Surprisingly, the one in his seat said "PILOT."

He quickly looked at the other three seats. The notebooks read "Co-Pilot," "Engineer," and "Navigator."

As Charley picked up his notebook, Blake walked up next to the co-pilot chair.

"I guess it's me and you. Don't worry. They'll be fine down there. They couldn't have picked two better people to stay back and lead the way."

Charley, ignoring Blake's optimism, took a minute to look around the cabin. Everyone was finding their seats and settling in. He picked up the notebook, sat down in the surprisingly uncomfortable chair, and turned to page one.

"This flight manual will walk you through the launch procedures. Follow them precisely."

Charley closed the book and Blake gave him a quick glance. Standing up on his seat, he peered through the windows that lined the cabin. His eyes could barely clear the window sill. As he strained for a few more inches of height, he saw them. His sister and the rest of the remaining walking up the steep slope out of the canyon. He could only watch them for a brief moment before his legs gave out.

Falling back into his seat, Charley and the rest of the crew began to pour over the manuals. Following the directions, with each of them taking turns flipping switches and turning dials, the ship came to life. It was a sound unlike anything Charley had ever heard. It was like turning on every computer ever built. The whirring of fans, beeps, and chatters. The whole cabin seemed like a living thing that was glad to finally be awake.

It reminded him of the time he had built his first computer. All the parts eventually found their place and made the machine come to life. It was the most beautiful sound in the world.

A few hours passed as the final pages of the manual came to a close. The last page had complicated details about oxygen levels and long distance sleep requirements, but at the bottom of the page, written in large lettering was the final instruction.

"Please put on your headset."

The crew pulled their headsets hanging from a hook on the side of their chairs. As they spoke through the microphones to test out communication, a distant voice was heard that made the crew fall silent. It was unfamiliar to everyone. Everyone except Charley. The instantly recognizable voice of his father.

"Charley? Can you hear me?"

"Dad?"

"Are you ready Son?"

"I am. Beka didn't make it..."

"I know..."

TWENTY TWO

After reaching the top of the ravine, Beka and the rest of the remaining turned to watch as the rocket began its final launch procedures. An alarm was sounding off in the distance, warning anyone close to the area to evacuate.

The engines began rumbling on the launch pad as the final harnesses and connectors linking the ship to Earth fell away.

The rocket was at full power within seconds, and with what seemed like all the energy in the world, lifted off the ground like a giant fire breathing dragon.

Beka shielded her eyes from the immense brightness of the blast as she tried to keep track of the rocket. It was covered in a thick cloud of smoke from the engines that soon engulfed the entire ravine. As the ship climbed higher and higher into the sky, Beka couldn't hold back the tears as she watched her brother, her only true friend, ascend into the blackness of space.

With everyone watching, straining to see the tiny speck of a once enormous ship, they began wondering what was next in their own journey.

Clasping hands, they turned around and began the journey back toward the city. Back toward the unknown and the uncertainties that lie before them.

ABOUT THE AUTHOR

Matthew Smith was born in Tupelo, Mississippi. He is an educator who lives in Sugar Hill, Georgia with his wife and son. He enjoys reading, writing, flying, and scuba diving.

Made in the USA
Charleston, SC
23 October 2015